Third in the Sir George *Series*

GOOD EVENING, SIR GEORGE

Yet More Tales of the Tinier Type

from

Donald Yule

Author of

Good Morning Sir George [2020] &

Good Afternoon Sir George [2021]

First published 2022

Copyright © Sandra Jane Donaldson 2022

The right of Sandra Jane Donaldson writing as Donald Yule to be identified as the Author of this work has been asserted in accordance with the Copyrights, Designs and Patents Act 1988

ISBN 978 1 3999 1104 7

Save for references to recognised historical characters and events and to actual works, locations, locomotives, ships, aircraft the events portrayed in this publication are fictional and any resemblance to persons living or dead is purely coincidental.

The copyright in the original text and the compilation of images and text resides in Sandra Jane Donaldson and her heirs and successors who reserve all rights. No part of this book may be reprinted or reproduced or transmitted or utilised in any form or stored by any electronic or other means now known or hereinafter invented, including photocopying and recording, in any information storage or retrieval system without the permission in writing from the author and publisher.

The author and publisher have made every reasonable effort to trace the copyright holders of material in this book. Any errors or omissions should be notified in writing to the publisher who will endeavour to rectify the situation in subsequent print runs or editions. Any mention of commercial products or brand names shall not be deemed to be an advertisement for or advocacy of such or imply any sponsorship of this publication.

Published under the auspices of Ingram Spark www.ingramspark.com. Cover design by Jessica Barrah www.jessicabarrah.com from an original photo of the classic view of Edinburgh from Calton Hill at sunset by Peter A Cordes and reproduced under the Unsplash Licence www.unsplash.com

Typeset in Baskerville Old Face and Tahoma by the author.

CONTENTS

Lots of Tales of the Tinier Type

		page
I	June 1999	5
II	May 2018	13
III	January 2021	27
IV	September 2009	31
V	May 1991	39
VI	September 2014	45
VII	July 2003	55
VIII	January 1879	57
IX	March 2005	67
X	August 2018	77
XI	October 2021	85
XII	February 2018	93
XIIA	January 2018	97
	Endpiece	107

BY WAY OF INTRODUCTION ...

... and explanation

As promised, this is the third collection of these variations on a theme of a titled protagonist which open and close with the same two words. Once again we will eavesdrop on conversations and rove far and wide across the years and the scenarios. As before, I have attempted to satisfy any curiosity aroused by adding some notes to the tale and thereby also acknowledging the sources who helped provide the factual trellis across which spread the tendrils of the Tale.

Over these "Sir George years", I have had the support, encouragement and occasional inspiration? from friends and family and others who surround my life which I once again acknowledge with thanks. Deserving of special mention regarding this volume are Ann Hunter of Thomas Tunnock Ltd of Uddingston [see Chapter V] and Kevin Boorman of Hastings Borough Council [see Chapter X].

In the Thanks department, I must also include Jessica Barrah for once again providing an eye-catching cover and the Office Staff and Carers of Apex Prime Care, Hastings, who made it possible for this elderly person to bring forth flowers of fiction from a well-nourished bed of fact

HAPPY READING!

DONALD YULE

St Leonards On Sea, East Sussex. donyule@the-pres.org.uk

JUNE 1999

"Good Evening, Sir George."
"Good evening, Mrs Braithwaite. How nice to meet you! Welcome to the Club! Do come through to the Bar."
Sir George was acutely aware of the lack of sincerity in his voice as he led his surprise visitor through to the Bar where he had been sitting contemplating how he should spend a rare evening in London. He had been musing whether to dine in the Club - either formally or informally - or venture forth in search of an Indian curry such as he never had with his wife, when the PA system sounded and he was summoned to the Reception desk.

Truth be told, back home in Gloucestershire he had been avoiding telephone calls from this lady whom his wife called "*That Yorkshire Person*". Now, presumably by some sort of detective work, she had nailed him and in the one place he had always seen as a haven. His wife had assured him that, in the last call she had taken from "That Yorkshire Person", all she had said to explain his absence was that he was "staying at his Club in London". Definitely no mention of which one!

Thus it was with a mixture of surprise and irritation that he led his guest into the comfortable Club bar, sat her at a table and duly provided her with a gin and tonic. It was the surprise element which predominated and dictated his opening salvo.
- I must say I am amazed to meet you here. You are a long way from home.
- I am at my sister's place in Woking. Her daughter's getting wed on Friday and she's been in a right tizz, so I had to head south. I've keeping up my work for the Group from there.

-My wife said you'd rung yet again. But I am sure she didn't tell you I was staying here.
-Rest assured Sir George – she did not. But, given the information still in the Public Domain about you, it wasn't difficult to work out where you would be staying.
-Yes. I've come up for the One Day International at Lord's tomorrow. Australia v Zimbabwe – don't really care much for either of them but an old Aussie pal from my City days has got a box and asked me along. It's a free day out at a famous ground so I grabbed the chance.
-Very Yorkshire!
 She was not the termagant Sir George had expected during the weeks when he had carefully avoided talking to her! He was looking at a petite, attractive and well-dressed woman. In fact, she was alarmingly attractive! *Heavens!* He thought. *What would people say?* Fortunately, there was no-one around who had recognised him BUT he knew the staff did. However what was this all about?
= You said work?
-As you must know by now, I've set up this group which we now call WAYS. That's Women Against Yorkshire Stereotyping.
-A rather catchy name!
-My husband thought it up! We had struggled to find a snappy name and he stepped in to stop us quarrelling. He's a policeman, you see.
Ahah! thought Sir George. *Maybe that's how she was able to track me down. A little bit of unofficial help!*
-But why me?
-You've got Yorkshire connections and I'm sure you can do something for me.
-If at all possible dear lady.

-I found out too that you're connected to the BBC and with you being a "Sir" as well and having been on television quite a bit a few tears ago, I reckon you can do your bit for Yorkshire.
- Well -
-Right! It's this television show Last Of The Summer Wine - if you know it-
-set in Yorkshire I recall.
-Exactly!
-I thought it was on ITV. Didn't know it was BBC. Haven't seen the thing in years.
-I can guarantee it's BBC and they should be ashamed!
-Is this to do with all this sex and violence we hear about?
-Anything but! NO! NO! It's just that it's unfair to Yorkshire.
--Good gracious! How on earth can that be?
-It's these ridiculous characters! They make a mockery of us Yorkshire folk.
-Indeed! I'm afraid you must elucidate further, Mrs -er -
-Glenda please!
-Well - er Glenda - what is it about these characters that is causing uproar in the Broad Acres?
-The programme is putting it about that Yorkshire folk are either daft idle men or terrifying housewives.
-I can see that would be an unfair generality.
-Happen! But Southern folk and the Yanks won't know different and that's where the money is.
-You mean tourists?
-Nay! I mean capital - investment for new businesses - for a new century - for a new Yorkshire - not just mills and terraced houses.
-I can see your point.
-Good. Then if you were thinking in investing in West Yorkshire would you be impressed if the first view you had

of the local workforce was from a TV show built around a workshy scruffy character like that Compo bloke.

-I do remember the character – a pantomime performance I thought -surprised he's still in it – not very appealing.

-And suggesting that is the type of person who's a hero to Yorkshire folk – well – what good does that do for the image? How can you square that nonsense with the fact that Leeds is becoming a major Financial centre?

-I can see there is a distinct image clash!

-I'll say! But can you do something about this? Can you get the BBC bigwigs to be fair to Yorkshire and get rid of the show – or get rid of the character?

-My dear Mrs – er – Glenda – I am afraid you must have been misinformed as to my connections with the BBC. All I did with them was to advise their Pension Fund some time ago. Then, I must admit, I did appear a few times on their News shows rabbiting on about money. But I have no connection these days.

-Then you're not a bigwig?

-Not a wig of any size I'm afraid. Can I ask how you came to believe that I had some sort of power at the BBC?

-My cousin Stan. He's no friend of us WAYS - made a mockery of us - but he did come up with the idea that I might contact you with your Yorkshire connection.

-There again. I was born in Yorkshire – which probably put the cricket into my blood – but we moved south before I went to school. I do have a cousin who has racing stables up in North Yorkshire.

-Should it be him I speak to?

Oh please don't contact him- he lives in a world bounded by Thirsk, Ripon, Northallerton & so on.

A sudden thought occurred to Sir George. *Ah! Tread carefully now* his inner voice cautioned.
-I hate to say this, Glenda, but this cousin of yours...
- Our Stan?
-Had you considered his motives for giving you my name?
-I thought it was very nice of him -quite out of character - and so I kept trying to contact you. Then when I rang your place in Gloucestershire and found you were in London and I was just down the line in Woking, it seemed like fate had intervened and perhaps we could meet. And I said earlier, it's very good of you and this is such a delightful place too.
-I agree. I've been a member here for years but ..
-There's nothing like this back home. I'm starting to see why people want to live in London.
-We were quite happy to leave after many years but - to return to your idea that I could somehow function as an ambassador for the views of your women's' group. Had it occurred to you - or perhaps your policeman husband - that this cousin, Stan, who doesn't exactly sound like he has your best interests at heart - might just have been playing a rather nasty little trick on you?
-Eh heck! Never! Oh - what have I done!

* * * * * * *

Sir George remembered afterwards that it was like watching a balloon deflate. He felt so sorry for this intensely locally patriotic person now in a state of almost collapse. With as many consoling and comforting words as he could find, he escorted her back to the Reception area and there found arranged that a cab would take her to Waterloo Station for Woking- the cost to put on his account - stayed with her till the cab arrived - talking as brightly as he could muster about the Club and its facilities - and then wished her well- with the hopes that the wedding would be a joyful day.

After the cab had departed Waterloo-wards, Sir George stood outside the Club's front door in a pensive mood. He decided he would chat with the Club staff but he felt sure the barman had heard every word of their conversation. He now had a twang of conscience: *Should he have invited the lady to stay for a meal?* Then he decided she had been in no mood for eating and she did say she was busy.

Unusually he found himself wishing Ill Will on a person. *That Stan* - he mused - *I hope something nasty happens to him!*

He would have a tale to tell on the morrow! So back to Plan A - head off to that little Indian place he'd been to on his last trip. He would have a GOOD EVENING

AUTHOR'S POSTSCRIPT

It is something of a mystery how a TV series which had no sex or violence in its scenes and never featured doctors, detectives or disasters should run to 295 episodes shown over a period of 37 years – all from the pen of the same writer, Roy Clarke. Not only that but more than ten years after its run ended, books are still being published and websites remain active for fans of *Last Of The Summer Wine*. The area around Holmfirth, West Yorkshire, where the many outdoor scenes were filmed, still attracts visitors with venues dedicated to the show and a coach trip available round the filmed locations. For opinions on all such I refer the reader to the interesting and informative [and copiously illustrated] *Last of the Summer Wine - An Appreciation;* Miles Eaton; [Amazon Imprint 2020] and to the earlier history: *Last of the Summer Wine;* Andrew Vine; [Aurum Press 2010] Both these titles suggest that the show did indeed attract adverse comment of the sort suggested in this Tale.

For many years, the episodes were built around the clowning and often OTT performance of the principal character, "Compo" played by the late Bill Owen [according to Eaton, success rather went to his head]. This is the character to whom Mrs. Braithwaite has taken exception here and she may not have been alone!

In a sad way, our Mrs Braithwaite's wish came true. Owen died midway through shooting Series 21 - which gave rise to three of Clarke's best ever episodes. Thereafter the show had a fresh style, helped by the inspired decision to bring in Owen's real life son to play the part of Compo's long-lost offspring. Those later episodes feature a large cast playing variations on the stock characters – often marvellously crafted - interacting via some very skilfully written plotlines. Add to that the quality of the dialogue, the brilliant comedic timing of the actors and the splendid scenery, then one can see how this harmless knockabout could indeed reach cult status.

[From amongst many memorable characters - the comic policemen Cooper and Walsh, "Electrical" Entwistle who is Chinese! -, this writer's favourite character is Luther 'Hobbo" Hobdyke – the fantasising ex-milkman brilliantly portrayed by Russ Abbott.]

The last ever episode "*How Not to Cry At Weddings*" was screened on 29th August 2010 but the series has been re-broadcast many times and is available to view on Internet channels. Watching those repeats, one finds oneself in a mobile phone-fuelled time-capsule of a quaint Yorkshire peopled by barmy old blokes and domineering females.

Watch it if you can – but beware! - it can be addictive.

MAY 2018

"Good Evening, Sir George."
"Ah! There you are," he replied, welcoming the young couple who had rather nervously joined him at the bar of his West End club. "Emma, Andrew, how nice to see you both again and in perhaps in more mutually congenial surroundings."

Almost immediately, there was a resumption of the rapport which, rather surprisingly, had quickly developed on the previous occasion. That had been a very grand Social Occasion at one of the minor Stately Homes on the Surrey-Hampshire border- described by the reporters who cover such events as "The Wedding of the Year" - at which both Sir George and the couple had been reluctant attendees.

The ceremony and festivity had taken its prescribed course and at some time after the raucous departure of the bride, Emma & Andrew had felt the need to escape from the alcohol-fuelled jollity of the braying mass inside the huge marquee on the lawns of the family estate. On venturing outside they found a fellow escapee, a small elderly gentleman, carrying a walking stick and propping himself up against the canvas tent wall behind which a tent pole provided support.
"Hello", Emma said. *"Not your scene either then?"*
"'fraid not!"
"Let me get you a chair, old chap", Andrew had offered and forthwith returned to the interior, leaving Emma and Sir George both rather awkwardly wondering what to say next. Emma hit upon a traditional solution.
"Sword or distaff?" she queried.

"Distaff, I suppose. I've known Guy and Venetia for years through business connections, so when they finally managed to marry off that daughter of theirs, they had to invite me out of politeness. Initially, I looked for an excuse but my friend Ralph persuaded me to attend -as he said - it would do me good to get out of London even if it were only down to the Surrey Stockbroker Belt."

"I think you must be in the same hotel as Andrew & I - I'm sure I saw you when we were checking in."

"Yes - thought it best - with all this formal dress palaver. Didn't fancy travelling on the train looking like some comedy act. How did you end up here ?"

"Venetia's is Ma's cousin so we HAD to be here! We drove down from our place out in Docklands and - like you - thought it best to use a staging point -. Ah! - Here's your chair."

At that point Andrew had returned carrying one of the rather heavy chairs from the marquee as if it were no heavier than one of the glasses of fruit cordial the two had been sipping.

"There you are old chap. Take the weight off your feet.. You're in our hotel aren't you?"

Having confirmed their common residence status they chatted happily for a bit, their conversation ranging over a far wider range of topics than either party had managed at their allocated tables at the sumptuous Wedding Breakfast.

Then Andrew suggested that as the day was wearing late and they had had their fill of the gaiety and perhaps Sir George had also, he might like to go back to the hotel - they could drive him -

Emma doesn't drink any more. Do you darling ? -

- Definitely not ! No, nay never no more .

Sir George agreed the transport suggestion and, after arranging to meet the couple where they had parked their car, went in search of his former business associate and Father of The Bride.

Emma and Andrew went to find Ma who was with Venetia. They found that the excesses of the day had taken their toll on The Mother Of The Bride for, when they mentioned they had been enjoying the company of a little old man with a walking stick, Venetia's explanation came out as:
Thassirgeorge - olfriend -you keep in with him - all alone - no kids - milti -mullionaire.
And as the embarrassed pair attempted to sidle away, Venetia grabbed Emma's arm:
- don'forgessirgeorge - finance your new biz
- and then - as they made for the exit, they heard her call something about their new companion being a *"Tinancial Fitan"*.

Sir George had been more than pleased to get a lift back to the little local hotel but had been disappointed not to see his new friends the following morning, as he was up and about early to catch the train back to London. In the ensuing days he was as usual busy with matters connected with his art collection but by a happy coincidence he met with Guy at a Board Meeting of an Investment Trust. Feeling that he should really send a thank you note to the couple and so hoping that he might get an address for them, he took the chance to query Guy about the couple.

However, Guy was unable to provide much information giving only the briefest of summaries:

*- odd couple –never met 'em before - she's Venetia's cousin's girl - very bright but some sort of personal problem– they have one of those little businesses that do all this clever software we use these days .
- Odd you say?
- well they seem to spend their time barging about on canals.
- I'll make a note to ask V to send you an address.*

Venetia's help, however, was not to be necessary as, a few days later, Sir George received a surprise phone call.

He recognised Emma's cultured tones at once.
- I must apologise for ringing you out of the blue, Sir George but it's Emma whom you met at that wedding the other week - if you remember?
- Indeed I did - you were the young couple from London - with whom I had the only conversation of the day - all the rest seemed only to talk about horses !
- Oh yes that's Ma's family all over.
Sir George heard Andrew call out
- Or the gear boxes in Land Rovers!
Sir George chuckled at the recollection:
- In neither case do I have much to offer in way of an opinion!
-Nor we either!
Sir George remembered with some pleasure that wide conversation involving the FTSE 100 index, currency fluctuations, the weather, the London Tube and the current state of English First Class cricket, all of which caused him to warm to the young pair and hope they might meet again. So it he was agreeably surprised when Emma asked if they might meet and found himself suggesting they met the following Thursday in the early evening. There would be no departure

from his established routine as it was a night when he regularly was out.

On his retiral from his senior position at the bank – now many years in the past and, as his friend Ralph described, *"laden with riches and honours"*; Sir George had realised he might be a target for persons seeking finance for commercial or charitable purposes. As a martyr to arthritis, he was never going to enjoy the open-air life he had espoused when younger, but his wish to avoid difficult meetings with supplicants had certainly contributed to his, albeit luxurious, hermit-like existence. Consequently, defensive strategies had become part of his life and he found that he had unconsciously adopted one in this circumstance. The last Thursday in every month was when he met up with Ralph for an evening's mild wining and dining and he was well aware of the date when making the suggested rendezvous to Emma. However, he found himself feeling a little guilty that he had arranged to meet knowing that he had a built-in excuse for curtailing the meeting if matters became embarrassing.

That guilt was still at the forefront of his mind as settled his guests down in surroundings that were clearly unfamiliar to them. Noting that they both requested soft drinks, he remembered something about their attitude to the excessive drinking at the wedding and found himself asking if they minded that he was having a gin and tonic. Then he came to the point and stated that he did not have much time as he had a regular dinner appointment. He was relieved to see the couple were quite happy to accept that.

Playing the host and noting that Emma was carrying a bulging document wallet, Sir George decided to smooth their way into the meeting.

"I assumed", he began, "when you rang, that you were seeking advice on some business matter. So I must tell you that I have very little connection with the bank these days but still move in financial circles - that's how I know Guy and Venetia."

"Ma did explain", replied Emma relieved to have been given such an easy entry into the exchanges. "But she thought that, as we had got on so well at that rather ghastly wedding do, it would be rude for us not to have a chat about what Andrew and I want to do , especially as matters have rather speeded up and there is a bit of pressure."

"Please go ahead. I'm intrigued. I understand you are in the Financial Software business about which I must say, I know very little."

Andrew stepped in.

"You will be relieved to know then Sir George, that it's not what we have in mind. We have in fact sold that business."

This puzzled Sir George: "You seem a little young to retire?"

"Oh. we're not planning retiring. We're - shall we say - changing direction."

Andrew continued: "Thing is, Sir George, we're both keen on an active lifestyle - we actually met as teenagers when doing the West Highland Way -"

"Which can be very arduous indeed - especially going over Rannoch Moor" - interjected Sir George.

Andrew moved into his PowerPoint Presentation mode.

"Not really. It's only really the first section which is difficult underfoot. And the section over Rannoch Moor makes use of the old Military Road so it's a problem only in really severe weather. We rather moved on from that."

18

"We've bagged all the Munros, " chimed in Emma.
"But our favourite spot was always The Rough Bounds of Knoydart" added Andrew.
Sir George threw up his hands in delight. "I knew we something in common!" he cried. For indeed he too, in his youth, had scaled many of Great Britain's highest peaks and walked its wilder remoter parts.
It dawned upon him that he was dealing with a couple who - like himself - relished a challenge.
"The open air was once my delight – though I never scaled all the Munros", he continued. "But the walls of the City of London closed round me and for forty years I sat at a desk and moved money, not my legs. I did it so well that my country rewarded me with a knighthood. In fact, I would have much preferred a new set of legs!"
The other two chuckled as they began to relax. Sir George was curious. "You plan to open a business in the mountains then?"
"Far from it, actually." Andrew was now keen to explain and leant forward. "We've been too far away from the hills and dales these last few years to indulge in intrepid adventures but we found we could get into the country on the canals. In fact we've decided that's where our future lies."
"Ah, I'm afraid I know little of canals though there was a picture of the Manchester Ship Canal on my office wall once. Apparently the bank had helped out with the finance at one time after some primitive attempt at Crowd Funding had failed. I rather think that's not what we are talking about here."
"Not exactly," continued Andrew. "It's the network of Inland Waterways which has rather seduced us and we've been given the opportunity to buy a small canal-based business."

It was Emma's turn, her voice now taking an enthusiastic tone.

"We had thought about running a marina – "

"Wait a minute", interjected Sir George. "I know about marinas. They're where you moor your yacht at the coast. I thought you were talking about canals which are inland."

"I can assure you Sir George, there are whole lot of inland marinas on canals and rivers – doing exactly the same thing- providing a service for boaters."

"Of course, of course. There must be. Forgive me! You speak of a world of which I know nothing."

Emma returned to her theme.

"Our first thought was: use the business skills we have come by to run a marina. However, on reflection we decided against, that. You see, we don't have marine engineering skills so we would be in management or hospitality roles. We don't want to end up running a canal side café - that's not the open air life we're looking for."

Andrew took over.

"We have been given first refusal in purchasing a going concern. It's a Fuel Boat business. Must I explain, sir?"

"Yes, please."

"These days, there are a lot of people who live permanently on canal boats. Mostly on traditional styled narrowboats. They're known as 'Continuous Cruisers'."

"That sounds rather hectic" opined Sir George. "Being permanently on the move - presumably, they have to stop to sleep."

"In actual fact – it just means licenced boat owners who don't have a permanent mooring. "

" Like gypsies indeed - and you will drive around them in a craft like an oil tanker?"

20

"Not exactly!" laughed Andrew. "We would certainly carry cans of diesel which a boater could use in an emergency but these boats have stoves for heating and cooking ..."

"So we would stock logs and kindling and coal for the stoves", interjected Emma. "Bulky stuff and not in a supermarket. And we would carry bottled gas for cookers ..."

" ... Not forgetting the toilet fluid!" added Andrew.

"As if..." came the swift reply in a tone of voice which suggested there was some history. "But you get the idea - Sir George. It's a world where your home isn't connected to the water mains or the sewers - you have to do that transportation yourself. And you haven't got mains gas or electricity - you have to solve the energy supply problems."

Sir George frowned.

"Bottled gas is a memory of camping days. This all sounds to me as though one was camping afloat. A rather spartan existence, I would have thought. Not one to appeal to many. Certainly not older people surely."

The two exchanged glances.

"I'm sorry to say you're rather wide of the mark there", Andrew said firmly.

Alarmed that her partner might be irritating a potential benefactor, Emma interjected.

"The canal boats we're talking about are like floating cottages. They mostly have stoves, yes, but they are electrically lit and powered. They can have central heating, a cooker, an oven, a fridge, a washing machine, a shower - all the amenities - it's definitely NOT life in the raw!"

"My goodness me! Thank you. I am duly instructed." Sir George's voice reflected his real astonishment at learning of a world of which he had no knowledge at all. However, the practised man of finance quickly recovered his composure, took a deep breath and assumed his best Chairman Of The Board's summing up manner.

"If I understand correctly from what you have told me - the enterprise you propose purchasing is one which supplies basic necessities. Always a sound basis for a business but I have to ask why you need finance. If I heard you rightly, you have just sold one business. Surely that will have provided you with capital. And if I remember correctly from when we first met, you have property in one of these new select areas of London."

Stern now in voice and manner Andrew explained:

"We were -as you chaps say - very highly leveraged – most of the businesses like ours seem to be – by the time we had paid back the money we owed – there was not as much capital left as we would have hoped."

Emma intervened: "To be scrupulously honest: next to none!"

Andrew nodded his head and continued: "What we are hoping to do is to rent out the flat, thus providing an income."

"A sound idea" opined Sir George. "It's your fail safe scheme really."

"And one which we don't plan to fall back on" replied Emma firmly. She tapped the document wallet and continued in the same vein.

"We have first refusal to buy what an accountant has deemed a Going Concern – we have the Accounts to prove it."

It was Andrew's turn. "And we have a proper Three Year Business Plan. It shows what funds we need and how they will be repaid. This IS a goer – believe me!"

Sir George found himself quite moved by the couple's enthusiasm but found he had nothing immediately to offer other than generalities.

"Your enthusiasm is most marked and the fact of your previous history in running a successful business venture is very much in your favour. You must have learnt that business success comes from having a decent product selling at a fair price and paying your contractors and suppliers on time" he intoned.
"I see a 'but' coming" responded Andrew with Emma nodding agreement.
"Perhaps" continued Sir George. "I have been greatly impressed BUT although I have very little to do with the Bank these days I DO know that this sort of investment is not really my Bank's business. If you had suggested buying ALL those Navigable Inland Waterways, then they might have been interested! I anticipate your disappointment."
Emma produced her prepared reaction.
"Ma did warn us that you dealt with huge schemes", she managed but Sir George had been thinking fast.
"All is not lost!" he cried. "Now I recall! There is some family money in a Beneficial Trust which could be put to use here. This seems to be the sort of enterprise which it could back - an ongoing concern and profitable in a small way. If you would kindly let me have your papers, I can take them to an accountant I know - clever chap called Framjee - who can put the figures under the microscope - so to speak. He knows more about small enterprises than I do - in particular, whatever amount they are asking for the Goodwill."
"That's terrific" chorused the pair.
With a broad smile, Sir George continued.
"I shall call you in a few days and arrange to meet up once more - this time for that dinner I think I promised you when I am entirely sure we can move progress. But before then

you had best contact the sellers and tell them the game's afoot."

So they parted, Emma and Andrew to return happily to their London flat – which they could now think of letting – and Sir George for his regular dinner appointment with his friend.

Sat in the taxi on his way to meet Ralph, Sir George mused on the meeting . Contrary to his misgivings his meeting with this enterprising couple had been very enjoyable. He would call Framjee in the morning as a double check but it would almost be fun looking through a set of business accounts and a sale proposal once more – he hadn't done the like of that in many a long year.

He felt a little guilty about making up a story about a family trust but his friend Ralph had so often pressed him as a single elderly bachelor to make arrangements regarding his considerable personal wealth and backing this venture would make a start. He was sure his former colleagues at the Bank could disguise his gift to the couple as being from a corporate entity.

So he had better get on with setting a Trust Fund! Though second thoughts suggested perhaps he would not make it publicly known as other distant family members might appear from the woodwork to plead for assistance!

Sir George rubbed his hands in satisfaction. It would be most enjoyable to tell Ralph about his decision to back the young couple's venture and to set up a Trust Fund. It might at last stop his friend's seemingly interminable lecturing.

It was turning out to be a GOOD EVENING.

AUTHOR'S POSTSCRIPT

Given the time which has elapsed between the pleasant meeting on which we eavesdropped and the date you are reading this, the Sir George of today might not be quite so ill informed as to life on UK waterways. He would know that Roving Traders, duly licenced by the Canal and River Trust [CRT], DO exist on Britain's network of navigable waterways and indeed such is the size and reach of such enterprises that they have their own Trade Association.

Sir George and his accomplice Framjee may well be able to help business purchasers Emma and Andrew in the matter of **Goodwill.** Classified by Accountants as an "Intangible Asset", the Goodwill of a business could be simply described as the excess of the money paid to purchase the business over the net value of its assets minus liabilities.

A rather hackneyed term, the **Stockbroker Belt** is a loosely defined region broadly defined to refer to any wealthy London commuter area or even as a generic term for any wealthy commuter suburb. The region takes its name from the history of affluent central London financiers who would commute in from these more rural neighbourhoods.

For the benefit of less active readers let me explain a few of Emma and references.

Opened in 1980, the **West Highland Way** is a 96 mile [154 km] Long-Distance Route running from Milngavie, north of Glasgow, to Fort William in the Scottish Highlands, with an element of hill walking in the route. The route snakes across **Rannoch Moor,** an expanse of around 50 square miles (130 km^2) of boggy moorland to the west of Loch Rannoch which remains an untamed wilderness. Generally this area offers relatively straightforward walking but in unfavourable weather, it becomes tough going as the route is exposed to the elements.

Knoydart is a peninsula on the west coast of Scotland. Sandwiched between Loch Nevis and Loch Hourn, it forms the northern part of what is traditionally known "the Rough Bounds". Because of its harsh terrain and remoteness, Knoydart is also referred to as "Britain's last wilderness". It is only accessible by boat, or by a 16-mile (26 km) walk through rough country, and the seven miles (11 km) of tarred road are not connected to the UK road system. Understandably, the area is popular with hill walkers, mountaineers and such types as Emma and Andrew and the young Sir George.

A **Munro** is defined as a mountain in Scotland with a recognised height over 3,000 feet (914.4 m). They are named after Sir Hugh Munro, (1856–1919), who produced the first list of such hills and at the time of going to press, the Scottish Mountaineering Club has listed 282 such summits and over seven thousand people had reported climbing all the listed peaks.

Apologies to those who attend weddings on the Surrey – Hampshire border – I am sure they can converse about matters other than horses and Land Rover gearboxes – important matters such as golf, holiday homes in the Dordogne, Preparatory Schools and so on.

JANUARY 2021

-Good Evening, Sir George.
-Hello Inspector. Good Evening to you too. Do come through. Leave the door on the latch. I'm sitting in my lounge.
-I trust I find you well, Sir George.
-As well as can be, given that I'm not very mobile these days. And in turn, I trust this will be the last of your visits.
-Indeed, Sir George and I must apologise, sir, for these most unfortunate events.
-Do sit down. It is a very pleasant view out over the grounds with the leaves off the trees. There's a contract gardening firm who do an excellent job. Though we didn't pick this place for the scenery, more for my late wife's need for a good Bridge Club!
-Thank you very much. It's very agreeable here - this Retirement Village - hadn't been to one before - you're usually a well behaved lot.
-I must apologise also, Inspector, for having to postpone your appointment but I had my Covid jab last Tuesday and the damn thing gave me a deuced awful reaction. The ladies who have tended to me since my wife died, absolutely forbade me seeing anyone.
-I quite understand. Very pleased you've been jabbed. Do you know when your second one will be?
-April sometime - if I live that long!
-Oh I'm sure you've got many years ahead of you!
- Thought that about my wife, Inspector! It all goes to prove Robbie Burns' warning about 'the best laid plans' still holds true. We took ages over finding a Retirement Home and no sooner had we got here, the wife took ill and died. Can't even

blame the Covid. Now I'm very much on my own as we moved such a long way. Might have to think about a move again. I can get in and out of bed and I can wash and dress myself but not a lot else these days.
-Bit hard on you sir, then, when a neighbour claimed you were the guy who molested her all those years ago.
-Whole thing was entirely preposterous - I had to dig through a lot of records to confirm but of course, I was doing my National Service before going up to Cambridge. I was at RAF El Adem in Libya when the alleged offence took place. I told your Sergeant that at the outset.
-I'm afraid that didn't help as she had trouble in understanding that information, sir.
-Well it was at the twilight of Imperial Britain if you like. We had bases everywhere - we ran Libya for a bit after the Second World War - took over from the Italians - nobody seems to know any history anymore.
- She sends her apologies for doubting you, sir.
- If I'd told your otherwise excellent officer that I was at RAF Luqa in Malta and RAF Habbaniya in Iraq also around that time, she would probably have decided that as my old Scottish grandmother would have said I was 'awa' wi' the fairies'!
-The lady was quite adamant. She'd kept a diary and she *did* work at the Hall.
-I don't really remember staff at the Hall. I was away at school, then National Service, then Cambridge. Then of course, the Old Man sold the place - and for a pretty penny too - it was a corporate HQ for a computer firm at first - some Japanese lot have it these days. And I still don't know which of my neighbours made those ridiculous assertions.
-I can tell you that she's not here anymore, sir. The family moved her to somewhere more suitable. She was making the

same sort of allegations about Harold Macmillan and Anthony Eden. Even my Sergeant spotted that was a bit unlikely.
-The matter is concluded entirely?
-Entirely. But − on another tack - I think you said earlier you'd been in the RAF.
-National Service. Seems so long ago. What a different world.
-You mentioned some overseas bases? And it's funny you should say that − quite a coincidence really − but there's names there I've heard my Dad use − El Adem and so on.
- He was Air Force?
- Regular. Must have been same time as yourself. He's on his own these days too. Might be an idea if you got together. I could give him your number if you like.
- I've got Carers in breakfast, lunchtime, teatime but if he could drop in when they've finished. I could certainly do with some company of my own background. My Carers are wonderful. They're considerate, compassionate, cheerfully competent and chatty *but* I can't have a serious conversation with them.
- That's just what my Dad says. He thinks nobody reads anything these days. Doesn't recognise anything on television as his world.
-Couldn't agree more. I'll expect a call from him. I'm sure we could have a GOOD EVENING

AUTHOR'S POSTSCRIPT

I must assure readers that Sir George when he listed those unfamiliar names was NOT "awa wi' the fairies" but recalling the days when UK had worldwide Defence commitments and, perforce, RAF bases in "faraway places with strange sounding names".

The "usual sources" will provide the questing reader with more detail but here is a summary:

- RAF El Adem was a base captured during WWII about ten miles (16km) south of Tobruk, Libya;
- RAF Habbaniya was about fifty five miles (89 km) west of Baghdad by the Euphrates river in Iraq;
- RAF Luqa was a Royal Air Force station located on the island of Malta, now developed into the Malta International Airport.

At the time when our Sir George was doing his (then compulsory) National Service, these bases were largely used by the RAF as staging points.

I have included this particularly tiny piece of fictional conversation to prove that I do not, as has been suggested, live entirely in the past and that current events do impact upon me. My sympathies to all those who reacted to the Covid injections, It was, of course, preferrable to the alternative.

This has also given me a chance to recognise the army of professional Carers whose unsung deeds do so much to bring quality of life to so many.

SEPTEMBER 2009

"Good Evening, Sir George."

Startled, the spoonful of Prawn Madras in my right hand froze mid-way between plate and mouth. I looked across the Indian restaurant in London NW2 to see the source of the greeting was the figure whom I had not really registered as coming through the door of the otherwise empty premises.

The face was more lined and the hair had thinned a bit but the "Sarf Lunnon" accent was the same and the tone of voice – that of someone who seemed determined to irritate you – still grated. Oh dear! I recognised someone from the past. Someone who persisted in addressing me in an unusual and wholly inaccurate fashion. He came into the body of the premises and stood a few feet away looking at me. I could scarcely ignore him or pretend I did not know him. *Here we go again*, I thought but I'm going to be firm.

"Stinker! Don't call me Sir George – we played that one out years ago in Clapham. There's no one in here to impress anyway."'

I was aware of using the well-practised tone of voice used for telling off subordinates. His reply, however, was equally firm. "And don't call me 'Stinker'! I'm not Simon Tinker anymore."

That rather put me on the back foot.

"You were when I saw you at Rosslyn Park – but - fair enough - that's a bit back now."

"Must be three years –since then I've become Simon Taylor – waited till Mum died and then got rid of the name she lumbered me with."

I felt my attitude softening.

"I remember wondering what Mrs Tinker was thinking about giving you an initial "S". I'm still Donald."
"What are you doing here?"
"Like you I suppose - I've come in for a curry. Most Thursdays, I get my shopping and food for the cat & then pop in here for Prawn Madras with pilau rice & a bottle of Cobra. "

"Only a Madras - never hot enough for me. I go for a Vindaloo or a Phaal if they've got one."
Déja vu all over again! I thought, remembering how, no matter what the item was under discussion, Stinker would interrupt your conversation to announce that he had a bigger, faster, or more up to date model.

Despite the recollection, I offered to move my shopping which was parked on the chair opposite me and invited him to join me. It seemed to be the polite thing to do although I had little desire to sit opposite this chap and was secretly delighted when he declined the offer, instead sitting at a table on the opposite side of room making the very polite explanation.
"No don't move your shopping bag - I'll do here- I meant- - what are doing in north London?"
"I moved here in the late nineties - went up in the world! Became Finance Director. It's good for getting into town down the Jubilee Line. Retired from that. Having great fun designing accounting systems. Are you living up here now?"
"Yes -over in Cricklewood -very swish little place - like you just done some shopping. You still go to Rosslyn Park?"
"Yes I'm part of the furniture. Bit of a beggar getting there on Saturdays though. I expect you noticed - Jubilee Line's

always closed – hope these damned Olympics will be worth it!"

I had no real desire to talk about our past acquaintance as I was beginning to recall the nature of the man but he had other ideas.

"We had good times back in the Clapham days", he began.
"Yes", I replied guardedly. "Lot of unforgettable characters."
I could see he had taken that as a cue to reminisce and he very quickly led me into an interchange .
-You were often with that little Scotch chap who was always cadging drinks – Wee Cocky Jocky.
-Wee Johnny Paterson.
-The very one! You used to call over to him – *Paterson, was it you or your brother who was killed in the War?* – never understood that – it doesn't make sense."
- Scottish joke
-Must be I suppose
- That Welsh chap who did the quizzes with you ...
- Evans the Quiz ...
- Yes – lovely chap– he said that Paterson had been your batman when you were in the Army. Rescued you when you were wounded with the Argylls in action in Aden.
-That's a Welsh joke
-I never understood that either. The pub was full of strange people – one chap set himself on fire – put his pipe in his jacket pocket when it was still lit
-Never to be forgotten
- Thing was - when your quiz matches were being played everyone had to be quiet – well there are a lot of pubs in Clapham , so I stopped going in.

A mental alarm bell started ringing at that point because that was *not* the way I recalled it!

Paterson, Evans and I had often thought that it was very likely that sometime, someone would get fed up with Stinker's irritating comments and punch him. Sadly, I was not present when that did happen but the other two were and they delighted in recalling the incident.

One of the regulars was a jolly lady of, shall we say, Rubenesque proportions who took exception to being addressed as 'Mrs Wobblebottom'. She had given Stinker, in front of the pub landlord, due notice of what would happen if the nickname were to be repeated. Stinker, of course, took no notice and on the following evening repeated his mode of address.

Although Evans and Paterson disagreed about how far back Stinker was propelled, both were agreed it was as good a straight right to the jaw as they had ever seen.

That was the last we saw of Stinker.

I refrained from mentioning the incident, though perhaps I should have done, as it seemed I had encouraged him. For the next few minutes as I shovelled away the curry and gulped the lager, Stinker treated me to an amazing rant. He obviously mistook my prioritising the consumption of food and drink for encouragement.

As I recollect, the thrust of his uninterrupted monologue was that he had an important new job running a little charity in Kilburn. I remember paying little heed to him but he had obviously picked up some knowledge of charity operations as he treated me to a synopsis explaining that one had to account for distinct types of funding. To be fair, he made a reasonable job of explaining the difference between Restricted and Unrestricted Funds but feeling he had to do this suggested he had forgotten what I did for a job!

I had cleared my plate and swilled the last of the lager when my antennae pricked up on hearing him say he was having trouble with the Accounting system and would have to get Price Waterhouse in to sort it.

Then, scenting the possibility of getting the sort of Charity Accounting Assignment that had become my speciality, I pushed my assessment of the man to one side of my mind - after all that punch to the jaw might just have shaken him into becoming a responsible citizen! I took him at his word.
More fool me!

I jumped in to offer my services: "Well, er – Simon - you've struck lucky - for that's what I do. I sort out accounting problems for charities . I cost a great deal less than do PWC. I can come and see you next week."

That seemed to stop Stinker in his tracks as he began mumbling about talking to the trustees and the conversation came to a halt with the arrival of the waiter to take Stinker's order and bring me my bill. This gave me an opportunity to escape.

I waited till he had given his order, noting that he copied mine, and then made to leave, giving him one of my business cards. He took it with fulsome thanks, mumbled some apology about not having one of his with him and, as I exited the premises, called out: "I'll ring you tomorrow!"

Later, walking homewards back along Willesden Lane with my bag full of tins of cat food and feeling most replete as usual, I realised I had very nearly been taken in by his story. I could have quite easily sat with him and attempted a serious conversation. I could have taken aboard his story but had remembered in time that this was a man who claimed to have played County Cricket for Somerset or Derbyshire – or was it both? - who said he was a qualified airline pilot who could no longer fly because of a rare blood disease he had picked up in the tropics - and many such like fantasies.

I felt that, as I had just avoided making a fool of myself while bringing back to mind happy days in Clapham before the walls of senior managerial responsibility had closed around me, it had been a GOOD EVENING

NOT THE POSTSCRIPT YET
- THIS IS A CODA

As you may have guessed, I never got that phone call but on the following Saturday, which was the first home game of the new Rugby Union season at Rosslyn Park FC, I ran into a pal from Clapham days .
 "I met old Stinker in Willy Green on Thurs," I began.
"Aha - I heard he'd run off somewhere up your way."
"Still calls me 'Sir George'!"
"Always was rather strange. Don't think he'd ever seen a chap in a blazer and club tie before! He seemed to think that you were a big wheel in English Rugby."
"Despite clearly being Scottish! Actually I don't think he could remember my real name. Did go on a bit!"
"No change there then!"
"Said he'd got a swish little pad in Cricklewood and that he's running a charity somewhere in Kilburn. Sounded rather fishy to me."
"Like him having played County Cricket?"
"Indeed! Was that before or after being an airline pilot?"
"Probably simultaneously! Who was it? Somerset? Derbyshire? He didn't seem to be sure."
"And didn't recognise my Middlesex tie! Anyway - he started to lecture me about Charity Accounting –"
" And you active in Charity Finance Directors Group!"
- Indeed! He'd obviously no idea what I did for a living! – I offered to help and he didn't half back pedal."
"I'm not surprised. Yes he's working for a charity – Diane and Caroline met him at Pride. He told them he's dossing down at his sister's in and volunteering at a charity shop!"
As John Paterson always said: *If you are going to be a con man – have a good memory!*

THIS IS THE AUTHOR'S POSTSCRIPT

Sorry but I felt I was due a look-in somewhere. Also this gives me the chance to honour the memory of two very loyal pals who have sadly since departed this world and to recognise the excellent work of the Charity Finance Directors' Group now morphed into the Charity Finance Group.

This Tale perpetuates the memory of years spent in a well-known hostelry in Manor Road in Clapham, South London and some of the larger than life characters who frequented it. Whilst the irritant, Walter Mitty-like "Stinker" is, I assure you, pure fiction, there lurk -as in all these Tales – elements of real life.

John Paterson – REAL: as was also our silly dialogue. To the question remembered correctly above, JP used to answer: *It was me – twice* -but the first time was an accident!
Evans The Quiz, Brian, - REAL: as was the quizzing life of the pub -it was where the Mind Sport of Team Quizzing was introduced to London – see www.qll.co.uk.
The auto- incendiarist -let us not bother with his name - REAL: I was present when that happened.

Of the foregoing, the hungry cat in Willesden Green is a very real memory and here he is. He was called Fluff.

MAY 1991

"Good Evening Sir George. Thank you for agreeing to see me. It is of course concerning the cottage."

"Good Evening, young man. Welcome to the Club and do let me get you a drink."

Sir George had not recognised the obviously very nervous young man who had been shown into the Club Bar. Neither had he picked up the name of this emissary from his London firm of Solicitors who apparently had sensed an urgency of which he had not been aware.

In truth, he felt he could have very well done without this interruption having had a long afternoon with his Financial Advisors undergoing microscopic investigation of all his investments. He considered the effort worthwhile but after a long weekend with in-laws, he felt quite drained and, on arriving at his Club earlier, had been rather irritated to find a message from his Solicitors awaiting him. Someone would come to see at 6 p.m. and this presumably was the "someone". But what was this all about? He settled his visitor with a soft drink and then started his interrogation.

- What is it that was so important that won't wait till tomorrow?
- It's Good News and Bad News.
- Give me the Good News first.
- It's something Wendy did for you.
- Your Office Dragon doing something for me!
- Wendy did indeed go to Scotland and as promised, has brought you a bag of goodies.
- My goodness - a firm of solicitors doing as promised without further ado.

-She has – I can vouch for this –she has waiting for you if you would care to drop in tomorrow perhaps – some Tunnock's Tea Cakes and some Scotch pies.
-My favourites! What a lovely surprise.
Sir George remembered a lengthy conversation with Wendy occasioned by his recognising her accent and his waxing lyrical about his days working in Glasgow and mentioning local foods of which he had become fond but found difficult to get in England. Wendy explained she came from Uddingston near Glasgow and would "she would see what she could do" when she was next "up home". Clearly that trip had happened and she had been true. to her word. The Young Man had an explanation.
-Well, some of us in the office did rather well from that investment tip you passed on.
-You didn't hear it from me!
- Confidentiality is our watchword but I think Wendy made a bit of a killing.
-My Financial Advisers are indeed very good and very thorough. It's where I've been this afternoon – I came here from Kent- where we've been over the Bank Holiday weekend and I'm staying overnight here – the wife drove straight back home.
-To Bournemouth?
-No! Eastbourne! I wondered last year if Wendy had got confused!
-That's Wendy all over! Being Scottish she gets very confused over English places. Heavens! There is rather a difference though and perhaps all this has been rather wasted effort.
-Now the bad news ?
-We've been trying to contact on the telephone you since last week and it wasn't till this afternoon that we hit base and

reached your wife at home. She was charming – and said you had important business in the afternoon but would be at your Club in the evening and gave us the phone number. We understood there was some urgency in getting your documentation signed and so decided to act ourselves -
-You didn't did you?-
-Well yes! I've went down to Hazel Tree Cottage on Friday.
-The premises in question! I thank you for your effort on my behalf but there was no need.
-You had impressed us with the urgency of the matter so I ventured forth out of London.
- It *had* been dragging on for months and I suppose I did set a deadline for eviction proceedings as the end of this month and it's the 28th already.
-Indeed Sir George, so I found I could catch a train which looked like it would drop me nearby and I thought there would be a bus and people who could direct me.
-But?
-Well I got to the station OK but found myself in the middle of nowhere with not a soul around, an unstaffed station and I was at a bit of a loss. I had the name of this cottage which Wendy suggested was near the Station – with the funny name I can't recall - it's between Tunbridge Wells and Hastings -but I had no clue of which direction and as I said there was no one about to ask. Fortunately, there was a dear old red telephone box there and luckily there was a card from a taxi firm so I called them –
-It would seem there is a role for these new mobile phones!
-We are getting one for the office, Wendy has insisted.
- It might have saved you a lot of trouble. But did you not have a phone number for the cottage?
-We couldn't find one. So needs must – I prioritised. Ventured forth! Thought I was pretty resourceful really.

- After a fashion! Though I must admit I've never been there myself. As you must know, at the end of last year - we inherited this cottage in a roundabout way from one of my wife's relatives in Kent. She didn't really know him - bit of an odd one out in the family. Single chap -very rich, but strange lifestyle.
-And strange how things can work out!
-It was quite a surprise - actually a bit of a nuisance as we don't need the place. Then we found we had inherited its inhabitant - this arty crafty Lingard chap - and your office couldn't find any sort of tenancy agreement. and obviously we wanted to put things on a proper legal footing. You chaps have drawn up a perfectly reasonable Agreement.
-All very right and proper Sir George and we are so sorry the matter has dragged on so long.
-My wife is happy with all your efforts at getting hold of the fellow but - as you must know -the phone at the cottage was cut off and he never answered letters. I wondered if Lingard was dead but there was nothing from the Kent Police. The wife even talked of going there - not all that far from Eastbourne after all! Then she thought of sending her sister who's a Senior Nurse at the hospital near Tunbridge Wells but I counselled against it - who knows what sort of madman this Lingard creature is!
-Best to be cautious in these matters!
-But you found your way there?
- Yes. Managed to get a cab. Wasn't far at all. Lovely cottage but no-one in. Looked all over for some sort of a note but nothing. Even went round to the back. Felt very adventurous. Wondered if I was going to come across some foul deed or other. Fortunately, I took the precaution of asking the cabbie to wait. He didn't know anything about the place at all - he

was from the next village apparently and the two places don't speak!

-How wonderfully English!

-Indeed. However, upshot is - I came back - waited for ages for a stopping train. Came back to the office having got nowhere and thought I should ring you. But, of course, you've been away.

-What about the place? Was it tidy? Garden - hedge - were they trimmed and neat? What about the windows? Had they been cleaned? You had a look around you said.

- Gosh! It wasn't neglected if that's what you mean. Oh! There was a ladder lying on the ground at the back - em - and there was some washing on a line - women's things - you know.

- Ah!

-And next door is very neat too - though here was nobody in when I tried the door.

A rather embarrassed Sir George had to make up his mind *Should I tell him?* was his immediate thought. *No - I'll let it go.*

Pleading a wholly fictional dinner appointment, Sir George brought the meeting to a cordial close shortly after with a heartfelt promise that he would commend the young man's efforts to the Senior Partner.

* * * * * * *

After his guest had departed Sir George remained for a few minutes in deep thought. *Had he dealt fairly with the young trainee? Yes,* he thought. He had not hurt his feelings. After all, he felt he had done something intrepid! And the firm of solicitors had gone out of their way to get a document signed for him. They hadn't needed to and if they could have contacted him would have known that. *My! my! This idea of portable phones might not be a bad one after all.*

What next? He would go into the solicitors on the morrow and let them know what he had not dared to tell the young emissary. He knew full well where the difficult Lingard was – in hospital after falling off a ladder! By chance, his sister-in-law was on duty when a person of ambiguous gender was brought in by the ambulance which a neighbour had summoned and she had recognised the address given as that of the cottage , now property of her elder sister.

More importantly he would see the generous Wendy and pick up his presents to take back to East Sussex. Presumably, he would be charged for the young lad's futile trip but how could he possibly object when Wendy had brought a bagful of his favourite Scottish food.

He decided he would go back to his room and ring his wife to suggest that whatever had been going on at Hazel Tree Cottage was none of their business and they could let matters take their course .

It had turned out, after all, to be a GOOD EVENING.

AUTHOR'S POSTSCRIPT

Just to note that the ubiquitous mobile has not always been with us! The first network was launched in Japan in 1979 with the first commercially available handheld mobile phone arriving in 1983. Widespread use in UK was clearly not in evidence at the time of this Tale.

There will be many readers who share Sir George's wholly understandable liking for the products of Thomas Tunnock Ltd of Uddingston, happily still available .

Following the Young Man's trail on the scenic Tonbridge to Hastings railway line is also recommended.

SEPTEMBER 2014

-Good evening, Sir George.
-Gosh! Still can't get used to being called that! Do sit down – er – do I call you "Doctor"?
-"Alice" will do quite nicely thanks.
-Splendid. Can I get you a drink?
-Just a still orange juice thanks – I'm driving. Ice and a slice as they say.
-*John! A still orange for my distinguished academic guest! Ice and slice. Put it on my bill.*
-I'd hardly say I was a "distinguished academic".
-As you wish but I was rather keen on advertising the fact to the hotel staff that my meeting an attractive young lady in the lounge bar was wholly to do with a matter up at the Hall.
-A cunning plan, Sir George!
-Please just make it "George" while there's nobody else about.
-I was surprised you're staying here and not at the Hall.
-Can't stand the place. Too many bad memories and anyway it got very run down in the months before the Old Man died. I wouldn't want to sleep there and certainly I wouldn't want to be waited on by that Gareth chap and his creepy little wife – no matter how good her cooking is.
-That would be the chap I spoke to when I rang last week?
-I imagine so.
- He was rather brusque.
-Well he is Welsh!
-So am I as it happens.
-Foot in mouth again George. Apologies!
-Well I wasn't wearing a pointy hat and carrying a harp.
-Apologies accepted. Ah – here's my drink. Thank you.

-My sister – she and her partner are at the Lodge – offered to put me up on their sofa bed – so help us. Hence I ended up here and it's remarkably good service. Though I suspect it's all a bit in the forelock touching tradition – we've been at the Hall for about a hundred years. Local squires, I suppose.
-But you were brought up to expect that role?
-Not at all. The Hall never really seemed like home. My parents were always abroad. My sister and I stayed there in school hols but always with a Nanny. So - didn't much like the place. No local friends. Happier at school.
-Unusual?
-Not where I was. There were a lot like me. I got on better there. It's not that I was any great shakes academically but I was a useful scrum-half and I captained the fifteen in my last year.
-But your father had a title ..
-My dear young lady, I was at school with the sons of Barons & Earls - and Generals - so mere succession to a baronetcy wasn't much – then when I started at the Bank I was the only one in my office not to have been at Eton – so I don't harbour any misconceptions about social rank
-But your family has long local connections then?
-Not into antiquity. We're from up north originally. Landowners there for yonks. Found some splendid seams of coal beneath the family seat in the 1880's – made a fortune - but, of course, the land around became industrialised so we found an impoverished aristo with a country estate down here, bought him out and moved away.
-And the title?
-Very Victorian thing too! In those days if you were a successful industrialist, you were made a baronet. Sort of halfway stage to the nobility. You're not a peer but you inherit the title.

-Very British!
-Indeed. And we did the British thing - went in at the right time - got out at the right time. Diversified as they say, because in the 1930's, we went into soap and cleaning things.
-People always need them!
-Exactly! And coal is a finite resource. Sooner or later you run out of the right stuff. And, of course, there's always been a frantic hoo-hah about closing mines. But you're Welsh - you must know about coal.
-Not a lot around Menai Bridge on Anglesey where I hail from.
-Oh foot in mouth again!
-Quite all right? They did in fact mine lots of copper on Ynys Mon - Anglesey -so we do have a historical connection with mining and the bridges to the island across the Strait are world famous. However, it was the Stone Age remains, first of all and then the Iron Age and Roman remains and Norman Castles in the area that really got me interested in archaeology. Which is why I'm here, Sir George.
-Yes of course! The Old Man did go on about Archaeology once on one of my rare visits. I'm afraid I would have ignored it like I ignored most of what he said in the years after Ma died. Always ranting on about my sister and I making unsuitable marriages. Only person he listened to was Gareth who was only the gardener at the start. But the staff moved out - don't blame 'em, the Old Man threw things at them - and Gareth and his wife moved in. Full time job looking after the Old Man, so the grounds got pretty run down. My wife reckons the couple were hoping to benefit in the Old Man's will and that Gareth seems to think so too. Looks like - they're going to be very disappointed. We'll sort something out for them somehow.

-There's a lot more than just the Hall and the grounds, I understand ?
-Heavens yes! Acres and Acres. Four farms. A real Estate. It's fine - run by a company for years - office in the village - just over the way .
-Ah yes that's where I telephoned originally they told me that the Hall's Grounds were outside their remit & that your father had died - which I knew - and you were now in charge - which I didn't.
- Indeed - for my sins - I find I am now Chairman of the Company that runs the Estate - how I shall cope with that I don't know -long way from my world of Negotiable Futures. I presume the office told you I was staying here which is how I got the call from Reception couple of days ago saying there was a "sort of a doctor lady" on the phone. I must apologise for a rather muddled conversation.
-We got there eventually and the upshot is that we get to talk about the dig.
-I have to say that of all the surprising things I've encountered here, the most surprising was having someone telephone me about excavating for Roman remains. Please explain.
-Simply - we believe you have a possible Roman site on your premises. We don't have a lot in this area, so the County Archaeologist and I are rather keen to dig - and as soon as possible.
-Exactly where are we talking about?
-There are some intriguing "lumps and bumps" in that paddock between the spinney and Long Lane.
-Oh yes! It's where Whatsername at the Stables grazes those tiny ponies. My sister and I used to play on those humps when we were kids. We knew them as the "Old Barns". I remember the locals saying Long Lane was a Roman Road.

-It almost certainly is. Not a famous one like Watling Street and so on but part of the network of minor roads and your site – just above the river valley -would have been a likely spot for a waystation. We did approach your father some time ago.
- I remember now. He got you confused with that TV programme Time Team.
-I gather!
-He was dead against it. Thought it was a fake! Mind you he thought all the quiz shows were fixed too.
-In the latter case he might not have been wholly wrong!

-But I'm not sure what to do. Normally in complicated matters I consult the wife but she's away visiting her family at the moment. Perhaps you should speak to my sister? I mean she's living on the Estate – or at least at present. She tells me that when we've settled everything she and her partner are going to move. They want to live on some sort of boat – motorboat which goes on rivers and canals apparently. Weirdest thing – I mean – I know people who live on houseboats on the Thames – but moving about –
- A narrow boat?
-No idea! Narrow? Given the size of my sister and her partner it can't be too narrow! But I thought canals were shut years ago.
- There's been quite a revival recently.
-Can't imagine why!
-Canal cruising is the coming thing. Boats can now sail freely through a tunnel under the Pennines.
- Whatever next! I know so little about this country! I can quote the GDP, exchange rates, Footsie 100 Index and so - on but – I'm too busy ever to get about.
-You're fixed in London then?

-Oh I get about but it's to Paris and Frankfurt or New York and Tokyo so I don't get much farther out of central London than Heathrow - I tell a lie! - I had couple of jollies last year -rugger internationals in Cardiff and Edinburgh - didn't see a lot of canals though - didn't even know they had tunnels.
-There is one in London!
-Gosh - yes! Near Lord's isn't it? I remember some chap mentioning it.
-Correct!
-Gosh, I know more than I thought! There must be lots of things to see on canals then?
-I think your sister and her husband will have quite a bit of scope.
-Ah there's the thing! You see, her partner isn't a husband. Something happened to my sister when she and I were young - never talked about it - something to do with a friend of the Old Man's - anyway she never wanted a boyfriend - the Old Man called her "his unnatural daughter". Shacked up years ago with another of her kind. Old Man let them have the Lodge but never spoke to them. He was like that. He never spoke to my wife you know - she's from Nigeria - though the fact that her lot are even richer than we are might have had something to do with it.
-The world has changed a bit.
-Don't I know it and it's all a lot of bother. Look I'm sorry but I don't see how I can let you start digging the Old Barns at present - there's just too much going on. Perhaps when we've sold the place the new owners will be interested.
-It's not Time Team you know - there aren't cameras and vans everywhere and hordes of spectators. You won't know we're there. I mean, the site can't be seen from the house or the Lodge and if you would let us use the gate off Long Lane, there would really be no traffic at all in the grounds.

-You have a very surprising persuasive way of speaking young - er Alice - you could do well in business. But still - it is one more thing in an ever increasing list. I don't really know.

-Had it occurred to you, Sir George, that if we find - as I am sure we will find - substantial Roman remains then the Hall and its grounds become immediately attractive to a potential American or Japanese purchaser?

-My goodness me! I hadn't thought of that! You have a business brain. Yes of course. Now you have put some value on your operation - it changes the whole picture.

-Does the picture say, "Go Ahead"? Shall I tell the County Archaeologist we're good to go?

-Why not? Why not indeed? I shall let my sister know - I'm sure she'll be pleased.

-We shall be in touch then. Thank you very much indeed.

- Well young lady - er Alice –this all shows distinct promise! What an unexpected pleasure it has been to meet you. I must say I'm fascinated by some of the things you said - not about your dig at the Hall alone but - if I heard correctly - you said you come from a bridge! - and then there's a canal tunnel under the Pennines! I wonder - would you care to dine with me - landlord's wife does a very passable risotto - food-wise I'm sure I can promise you a GOOD EVENING.

AUTHOR'S POSTSCRIPT

British Canal enthusiasts, whether boaters or gongoozlers will doubtless have shouted at this rather dim Sir George explaining:

(1) to enter a narrow lock on the Narrow Canal system, a craft must be under seven feet (2.13 m) wide, so boats tend to be just six feet ten inches (2.08 m) wide hence the term, [Broader craft are "wide beams"]

(2) The 5,451-yard (4,984 m) trans-Pennine Standedge canal tunnel in northern England was opened in 1811 and though closing in 1943, re-opened to leisure craft in 2001.

Our protagonist's father also seemed out of step in his regard for the TV Series "Time Team", a Channel 4 programme that ran from 1994 to 2014. Created by television producer Tim Taylor and presented by actor Tony Robinson each episode featured a team of specialists carrying out an archaeological dig over a period of three days, with Robinson explaining the process in lay terms. With 2.5 million viewers at its peak, the series brought Archaeology to the notice of the viewing public and it was revived on the YouTube Social media channel in 2022 with several of the experts returning.

The Welsh lady archaeologist of our Tale claims her origin to be "Menai Bridge" which I can assure readers not familiar with the geography of North Wales, is a small town on the historic Isle of Anglesey in north-west Wales. Known in the Welsh Language as *Porthaethwy*, it overlooks the Menai Strait, the narrow strip of water dividing the island from the mainland and is within sight of Telford's 1826 Menai Suspension Bridge - from which we get a clue to the English place-name.

Yes! Alice did say "bridges"! The area is not content with one historic crossing – it has TWO! The necessity for a rail link to Holyhead - a port which served Ireland -brought forth the noteworthy Britannia Bridge. Designed by Robert Stephenson, this was a tubular bridge of wrought iron rectangular box-section which opened in 1850. This construction was destroyed in a fire in 1970 and the crossing was reborn in a 1974 as a double decked road and rail structure finally operating as such in 1980.

Given her childhood exposure to artefacts ranging in age from prehistoric times to the Industrial Revolution one can well see how Dr. Alice was influenced in her choice of career!

Hang on! There might be a bit more to this!

MORE TO TELL?

It may seem that this Tale was rather quick to rattle up against the buffers of the perennially pedagogic Postscript. You may feel that there is more to tell, such as:

- Did something happen between the middle-aged rich City Financier and the attractive young lady archaeologist after their dinner *à deux* at the country pub?
- Did Gareth produce a Will in which everything was left to him?
- What happened at the Dig? Are they really Roman remains?
- What happened to the sister? Did she and her partner become boaters? *[And have they been posting videos on Social Media of their adventures and misadventures on their no-doubt expensively equipped and quirkily named narrowboat?]*

I shall leave all that to you Gentle Reader – after all, your stories are the best.

JULY 2003

Picture, if you will, your humble author in the above month and year, at a time of day appropriate to the title of these Tales, sitting in a pub within walking distance of Waterloo Station, London. Suddenly one man with a briefcase in one hand and a glass of whisky in the other encountered another similar. Both were entirely oblivious of the author's presence and interest in their conversation!

--Good Evening, Sir George.
-Ian! Good Heavens! I've not seen you to speak to since- how long?
-I can tell you Geordie man! Not since the Sandstorm affair.
-Long ago as that! My!
-I've caught sight of you plenty times - in the City - on the Drain - but the last time we spoke was when we were wriggling out of Sandstorm.
-Haw! I'll not forget that in a hurry! Could have cost me the career and the marriage and you would not be now calling me "Sir" George! What brings you here?
-Oh I've been discussing my forthcoming retirement and - more to the point - my forthcoming pension. All seems OK so I thought I'd drop by for a swift one before I face the train home. Will you be having another?
-Not for me thanks Ian. I've got one further wee call to make over the road before I can hit the tracks. You'll have made it to a good rank!
-Cannot complain at all -see!
Your auditor could not see but we can assume some evidence was proffered..
-Well done - well deserved! You'll have earned a comfortable retirement.
-A policeman's lot becomes a happy one when he retires!

- Wife ok?
-Greatly involved with village life. She was the one who spotted your knighthood. Belated congratulations! Your lassie?
-Still mad about horses. Teaches dressage these days. I often think of the Sandstorm time. We were both pawns in a much larger game. A bit lucky in the end.
- We could have been made scapegoats but we weren't.
-Because - of course - we kept mum and none of those English lads ever spotted we had done our Accountancy Training together! Tae auld acquaintance!
-Auld acquaintance! -Look I have tae gang but we must meet up for dinner -with the wives of course. Damn good place near us. Some good malt considering it's England - do you still like the island malts? I'm sure you'd like the place. Aye Ian laddie- we could have a GOOD EVENING.

AUTHOR'S POSTSCRIPT

Savvy readers will have recognised the codeword "Sandstorm" in the foregoing and know we are harking back to the days of the BCCI Financial Scandal about which I shall make no more comment. "The Drain" is an old City hand's nickname for the Waterloo & City underground line. [You can work out where it runs!]

It will not have taken too much intellectual oomph to spot that we have eavesdropped on two Scots old acquaintances and we can guess one is a banker and the other on the brink of retirement from the Fraud Squad or some such investigative body. The matter is best left there!

JANUARY 1879

Dear Reader
This Tale is from the Age of Empires when developed nations conquered the lands of less developed mainly by the use of superior military technology. Consequently you may see reported views and opinions which do not hold currency today but are presented here as indicative as those of the time.

Travel back then to an evening when sun was sinking over a small township in the hinterland of Natal Colony, southern Africa. We are about to eavesdrop on a conversation between two young men, one far travelled the other less so but more motivated in his quest. The former, lost in thought and smoking a pipe of tobacco on the veranda of the only hotel, had not heard the latter - a man of sturdy build - approach and was consequently surprised by the greeting which came in locally accented English:

-Good Evening Sir George.
-You startled me sir!
-I must apologise but the hotel proprietor pointed you out to me.
-May I ask your name, sir?
-Schoeman. Piet Schoeman. Like yourself not a resident of Natal Colony.
-But you are Cape Dutch by the cut of your jib!
-If you wish. My family is certainly from Cape Colony.
-I thought all the Cape Dutch migrated north years ago.

-A lot did but my family were making too much money selling horses to the British, so they stayed put. Most of us did.
-Are you by any chance here selling horses? I need a fresh one if I am to get to the country beyond the Buffalo River.
-You could be out of luck, man. All horses and carts have been commandeered. Myself, I have found it difficult to travel.
-My horse has not much left in her and the Innkeeper is not willing to lend his horse and wagon for a trip to Zululand. All the tracks will be damaged by wheeled traffic to the Buffalo River and besides, he needs the tackle himself to bring supplies up from the coast.
-I too intend to travel to the Buffalo and beyond in the tracks of the Army. But I am not in the horse trade and have only sufficient mounts for myself.
-You are not prospecting for minerals?
-No indeed, I am a journalist and I believe there's a story to be had with Thesiger's - sorry, we must now give him his title - *Lord Chelmsford's* advance into Zululand - for which I appear to have arrived too late. May I in turn enquire what an English milord is doing in the wake of an invasion?
-First - I am not what you call a "milord" though our innkeeper - admirable fellow otherwise - seems convinced I am a peer of the realm.
-But you are addressed as "Sir"?
-That is because I inherited a Baronetcy from my father. But it doesn't make me a Peer of the Realm.
-This is too complicated for me.
-It was for Father too, poor chap! He no sooner got his Knighthood - for *bashing metal in the Midlands* he called it! - than he was struck with an apoplexy. One minute his usual angry noisy self - next minute he was gone - apparently.

Rotten shame really and it all happened when I was on my travels.
-In Africa?
- I am but lately arrived in Natal Colony.
- You will presumably wish to return to England presently?
-I shall have to. There is but my mother and younger brother there to look after our interests. He is, I regret to say, of a flighty disposition - lives in London -interested only in sport.
-He is into horse racing?
-Only slightly I think. No, his time is given to these growing team games – cricket and rugby football.
-This is a land of farmers, hunters, and fishermen. Busy hardworking people. I don't think your English sports - your cricket and your football - will ever catch on in southern Africa.
-Perhaps not. I am but slightly acquainted with team sport as my family felt I was best served by seeing the world.
-You have clearly done that by coming to this far off land.
-More than that! I was but lately in North America - the United States - splendid place for a young man to be these days.
-A rapidly expanding country so I hear –
- very much so! I fear I may have missed a chance there - couple of years back I wandered into their Arizona Territory and bumped into a very go ahead prospector chappie called Ed something or other- he was actually setting up a township – I thought nothing would come of it – it appears I might have been wrong there Hey ho!
-And what brought you from a land of opportunity to this end of Africa?
-I could have easily stayed in America but in theory I am furthering my family's business interests and they felt that I should explore southern Africa instead. They cabled me and

sent me on quite a journey- which I have to say has been quite an adventure.

- and your business?

- We are a manufacturing firm in the English midlands and we make picks and shovels

- Good to have if you're a miner or indeed anyone opening up country. I don't see any samples.

- Well no that's not what drew me up here. I have a cousin in the Army- I tried it but couldn't put up with it - nobody would listen to a word I said. However, he stayed in the 24th Foot - that's a regiment which recruits from our part of England - Warwickshire - and of course they're out here. And I've come all the way up here and missed him. Nobody can say that I didn't try my best.

-You've done well and -by the way -"not listening" is not confined to the Army young man! That's what I like about journalism -people DO get to hear your opinion - even if you're off beam

-I take it you are keen to reporting on the advance into Zululand?

-Indeed. Like you I am trying to catch up with someone. My family back in The Cape are friendly with some German speaking people - the Adendorffs. One of them knows a lot about Zulu warfare and - I believe he is with the local volunteers. I think that where he is, the action will be.

- And that action is likely to be what?

-Thesiger - though I should really call him Lord Chelmsford now - is obviously taking a chance. Based on his recent success against the tribes on the frontiers, I think he is expecting a quick result. So that by the time his despatch informing London of his invasion actually reaches the government - 20 days or thereabouts - it should be all over in Zululand.

-Indeed? My estimable landlord has suggested to me that the Zulus are a different proposition to the other peoples?
-I've heard that also and I believe it. The rule would be: *Don't get caught in open country because the Zulu tactic is to surround and overwhelm by weight of numbers.*
-I wasn't in the Army long but I would agree with that! That's the sort of thing that happened to Custer when I was in America.
- I would think that provided you fortify positions like river crossings, sheer fire power would destroy any attack by barefooted tribesman armed with only a shield and spear – no matter how brave they might be. And from what I heard via Adendorff; these Zulu people ARE ferocious! They will attack even if their leaders tell them not to!
- In that case, presuming also we have cavalry, we can irritate them and get them to run after us and lure then into the range of the big guns.
-You're talking like a soldier now!
-Must have learnt something then!
-And Thesiger – sorry, Lord Chelmsford – must know all that too.
- I am sure he will not split his command in an area when up against an unknown number of hostile tribes like Custer did.
- And I will have a story about another victory for British arms. But what about you? With no horse, you will not able catch up.
-It appears so! I can tell the family I did my best to meet up with the cousin but that a war intervened. Even my mother would accept that as an explanation! The landlord has suggested I leave my old hack here and get a lift back to the coast. His boy is taking their equivalent of pony and trap back down there for supplies tomorrow and it was suggested I go along.

- I think that is your best plan. If you like, I could take a note to your relative in the Twenty Fourth. I am sure I will catch up with them.
- I am obliged sir. I have my writing case and materials and I am sure I can beg an extra light of the innkeeper. Yes indeed I shall to that task and turn around in my tracks - in fact, it seems time I headed back to England!
_ And time for me to see to see to my horses. I bid you good night and promise I shall take your note in the morning.

* * * * * * * * * * * * *

After the African had disappeared into the twilight, the young baronet remained on the veranda in pensive mood.

His mind turned to his childhood and Nanny Ponsonby whom he often recalled as the only person who ever listened to him. He remembered her words: *You'll go far Master George.* Well he had done.! Across Europe at a time when two of its nations were at war; across the Atlantic to see a new country in the building and now to southern Africa to witness an outpost of Empire struggling develop. Yes, when the family had sent him packing, the pretext was that he would go to where new mines were being developed and survey the potential market for his family's picks and shovels. He could certainly report that there was a likelihood of a mining boom in Arizona Territory. *Would there ever really be a town called Tombstone? Unlikely!* he thought. And what would he say of the future for this strangely beautiful country? After these apparently savage peoples were subdued who could tell? So although he would not be reporting a meeting with his soldier relative at least he had made contact if indirectly and surely there was no need to worry about the two battalions of the 24th Foot who seemed to be an experienced bunch with competent leaders. Time to go home then.

Home and back to his Mother - *would she still try to dominate now he was head of the family?*

Was his young brother still living in London? Was he still only interested in sport? Was he playing cricket in Lord Rosslyn's Park in Hampstead? Cricket? Perhaps he too might play again, although on reflection he remembered the arguments that had ensued when he used his leg to defend his wicket.

What else had he heard about his brother? Oh yes! The cricketers in Lord Rosslyn's Park were thinking of forming a club to play some code of football. That did seem rather unlikely. Most of all -maybe now he was head of the family, people would listen to him.

In the meantime, he had a letter to write to give to Schoeman on the morrow. and there was the prospect of the promised platter of cold meats. He took a last look out at the lightning still crackling on the horizon then turned indoors. *Perhaps there would be a bottle of beer with his supper.* A thought occurred to him: *If the army were to be engaged against barefoot warriors, could they not fortify their position with a line of broken beer bottles?* He would suggest that in his letter. Sir George clapped his hands in satisfaction with the turn of events.

It had been a GOOD EVENING

AUTHOR'S POSTSCRIPT

Enough has been written about the events which followed the conversation in our Tale - which must have taken place one evening between the 11th and 22nd January -and indeed epic films have been made based on those events. This Addendum will be confined to merely elaborating on the remarks made, opinions expressed, ideas mulled over by our two protagonists. I shall leave readers to keep the score on how accurate their predictions turned out to be!

The 24th Foot was an infantry regiment of the British Army dating from 1689. It had a variety of names and headquarters prior to becoming the 24th (2nd Warwickshire) Regiment of Foot in 1782, being based in that English county and recruiting from Birmingham and surrounding industrial towns - the home ground of our Baronet. Although based at Brecon in South Wales in 1873, contrary to the impression given by the epic 1964 film *Zulu*, it was not predominately a Welsh regiment at the time of our Tale.

The "Ed" whom Sir George met in Arizona was presumably prospector Ed Schieffelin who *did* found a township based on the local silver mines which became a famous boomtown and was indeed called Tombstone, perhaps best remembered today as the site of the Gunfight at the O.K. Corral.

Frederic Augustus Thesiger, (1827 –1905) was appointed to command British forces in the Cape Colony in February 1878 with the local rank of lieutenant general and in October succeeded his father as 2nd Baron Chelmsford. He brought the Ninth Cape Frontier War to its completion in

July 1878, and was made a Knight Commander of the Order of the Bath in November 1878. There is an opinion that his experiences fighting against the Xhosa speaking peoples created a low opinion of the fighting capabilities of African soldiers which later led to the well-documented and oft related disastrous consequences during the Anglo-Zulu War. At the conclusion of that conflict, Chelmsford was relieved of his command and never commanded an army in the field again. He was portrayed in the film *Zulu* Dawn by Peter Finch.

From the late 14th to the late 19th century, *apoplexy* referred to any sudden death that began with a sudden loss of consciousness, especially one in which the victim died within a matter of seconds after losing consciousness Today we would call it "a stroke".

There were many people named Adendorff but it sounds as though the one Piet Schoeman was looking for was Gert Wilhelm Adendorff [1848 -1914] who certainly was where the action was that month! A lieutenant in the Natal Native Contingent, he seems to have been the only soldier on the British side present at both the Battle of Isandlwana and the Battle of Rorke's Drift.

As to his thoughts about cricketers playing in Lord Rosslyn's Park being unlikely to form a football club - wrong again! History tells us that under Mr. C B Hoyer Millar's leadership that most certainly did happen and in the year of our Tale too. The outcome can be seen today by anyone travelling along London's South Circular Road between Putney and Richmond in the well-appointed premises of Rosslyn Park FC where the shape of the goalposts show which code they decided on.

Sir George was, of course, not the only person in the history of the game of cricket to encounter problems when the ball struck the batsman's pads!

Lastly, there IS some evidence that the British Army at one of its fortified posts in the conflict against the Zulus did indeed use a line of broken bottles as a means of defence!

In compiling this Tale, I have been inspired and aided by reference works on my bookshelves, in particular:

The National Army Museum book of the Zulu War, Ian Knight [Pan Books 2004]
Rorke's Drift, Michael Glover [Wordsworth 1997]
One Hundred Years of Rugby Football – A history of Rosslyn Park Football Club 1879- 1979, Rex Alston Ed. [Rosslyn Park Football Club 1979]

MARCH 2005

"Good Evening, Sir George"
The greeting was that of the Reverend Charles Warburton who had let himself into the Church Hall by the back door and walking through into the main hall, now witnessed Simon Buckley carefully placing the portrait of his Victorian industrialist ancestor on an easel at the side of the stage and thus felt he should pay his respects.
"Oh hallo Vicar! Thanks for agreeing to have a chat before the Meeting", came Simon's cheerful welcome.
"Not at all dear boy!" The clerical gentleman made his way up the side stairs and onto the apron stage where Simon had also set up a lectern. "It is as well to be briefed before a meeting of this import."
AUTHOR INTERVENTION: We have two characters, SB and CW, on a stage – let's make this a "play for voices" with sound effects, as necessary.
SB   I thought that it would add a sense of atmosphere if we had our family picture of the old rascal who built the railway in the first place. So Ruth and I dug it out and dusted it down. It really doesn't fit the décor in our place.
CW   You might also have brought a picture of Doctor Beeching who closed it!
SB   To be fair, Vicar, it was on its last legs by 1963.
CW   And we are lucky to have the station premises and our few yards of track remaining and a successful young modern businessman like yourself so involved in keeping activities alive in and around the old station.
SB   It's lovely place even if Peter Davies has stuck his adverts everywhere.

CW   Davies THE Decorator! Did you see that someone had scribbled on one of those boards: 'No job knowingly under invoiced'?

SB   But we must agree his chaps have done a wonderful job and our little tearoom is always bright and sparkling. A great attraction on Sundays when we open - and Betty's scones of course! But a lot of that has been down to you, Vicar, with your contacts in the Railway Preservation world.

CW   But alas, all I could persuade to come to this corner of Cheshire were the gang who own that smelly diesel and the guards van that have no connection whatever with the North of England.

SB   But we shall have steam again and five miles of track when tonight's meeting sets up our railway company!

CW   With the Lord's blessing.

SB   The Lord in this case being Mister Moneybags Harris, our self-styled Lord of The Manor!

CW   Now Simon, 'the Lord Giveth and The Lord Taketh Away' - Book of Job Chapter One, verse twenty one.

SB   You've a habit of saying that Vicar and I've checked up! It's not quite right.

CW   I forgot you were an Oxford man, Simon.

SB   Indeed. But your point is well made and you could add 'But not in equal proportion' otherwise Ruth and I would be in The Hall now and not Ted Harris. That portrait is almost all that's left and we're fed up looking at the smug old beggar. When we have that grand opening day, Ruth and I will grandly donate the dam' thing to the railway!

CW   And by so doing, you will be tacitly acknowledging that you and Ruth in setting up your hi-tech business here have done very much the same as old Sir George there when he set up the silk mill back in the eighteen eighties.

SB   As you wish - but we have a meeting shortly ..

CW I trust the track bed – so-to -speak – is in working order.

SB The chairs are all out as you can see and Ruth ran off the agendas earlier. If we get that number it would be very welcome. The mike is working and that noise you can hear through in the kitchen is the noted Betty from Betty's Cakes and Teas and everything else.

CW... where would we be without her?"

SB And vice versa! She does very well out of running our tearoom on Sundays and if – sorry – when we become a proper fully open railway – she'll do even better – and I think this is her!

Noise of a roller shutter being opened. BETTY enters conversation calling across the Hall.

B Good Evening Vicar, Mr Buckley – Oh I like that picture! Is that the great Sir George?

CW Hello Betty – yes that's the great man – is all well in there?"

B Well Vicar, I wish you would have a word with the Hall Committee about the tea boiler - it's on its last legs. On the other hand you could have a word with God – that would probably get things sorted quicker!

CW I shall bear it in mind dear lady. Have you got help?

B Oh yes thanks. My sister and her daughters - I hope they haven't rushed their Homework again – we'll be all right if the boiler stands by us. I only interrupted to ask how long do you expect the Meeting to last?

CW Shouldn't take long. Simon will describe the re-opening of the line from the existing station premises as we have shown on his map over there. Then all we have to do is propose the formation of the new railway company. Oh and how we will need more volunteers. But half- say threequarters -of an hour - if nobody objects - and we'll get going prompt at seven thirty - I'll open the doors shortly.

B   Right we'll work to that - and Vicar, you won't forget my little word with you will you?

CW   Indeed not. Thank you Betty.

Noise of shutter closing then footsteps and creaking of stairs as the heavily built TED HARRIS makes his way up on to the stage.

CW   Ah Mr Harris - you rather startled us by coming in that way - but a very pleasant surprise.

TH   Aye! Good Evening both. Mind if I join you up here? Sorry to startle you Vicar! My businesses have supplied the locks for every Church and Parish Hall for miles around so I have a key to all of them. Thought I would have a word with all of you before the Meeting - just to be sure and I didn't want to draw attention to myself.

SB   We're very pleased to see you. The other Trustees will be here in time for the advertised start but, of course, they've all got to come from Manchester, Liverpool - Birmingham even.

TH   I see Sir George is here. We've got one a bit like that up at The Hall - he built that too, along with the old Mill, the railway -half the present village. You've done well to put that out - it will remind everybody where we're coming from. Sharp looking lad! No wonder he made all that brass. And that huge map at the back of the hall - I take it that's the plan of the line - as was in the local paper last month?

SB   It is indeed - I put it there so everyone could have a close look.

TH   Good, good! Well you know I think you've got a good idea . I don't want to be part of this meeting but I just wanted to check a few things.

CW   By all means.

TH   You've got a good little set up here round the old station. You run your Station Trust and your Preservation Society soundly and you've got that little train shuffling about on a Sunday - with that Decorator lad, Davies, running the diesel ..

CW   Smelly thing!

TH   A lot of things my businesses provide are smelly but they make money, Vicar and it's all I can see you've got at the moment. I just want to be sure you've got your next step right before I give my backing.

SB   Very simply - we form a charitable company and relay the track bed for five miles and run a line which will play its part in preserving the railway heritage of this part of Cheshire.

CW   And we set up an appeal for funds.

TH   Lofty ideals!

SB   Indeed but it works elsewhere and there is absolutely no reason why it should not round here.

TH   And what sort of railway are we going to end up with?

SB   Single track as it was all its days.

TH   But not all the full line surely! How would you cross the bypass?

SB   We shall have to terminate there, sadly. But it is five miles and quite enough track to be looked after by us and give a good visitor ride there and back.

TH   Fair enough. But - it's long time since a train ran down that track.

CW   Indeed. It is time we had the sound of steam again.

TH   What I mean is - is it sound? There must be a bridge or two?

SB   We have had a proper survey done. There's really very little engineering on the route. My ancestor's lads knew what they were doing - it runs just below the crest of a small ridge all the way. A couple of Public Footpaths cross the line but no roads until you come to the bypass and we can do nothing about that at the moment. The only bridge is where we cross Sandy Brook and the surveyors reported it to be rather "over engineered" - could have taken mainline trains - maybe that was part of some grand scheme back in the day.

CW And maybe it is the Lord's Will that it will happen one day under our guidance.

TH But you'll need rails and whatsits - sleepers that go under them and it's all on gravel. None of my companies sell those.

SB Not to worry. We're part of a community and we've got that organised. And my organisation can help financially. Tax efficient say my accountants.

TH Sorry to keep going on but I just want to know you've thought of everything. At the moment you've got use of a diesel shunter and a van. That strikes me as not enough.

SB Correct! It isn't - though we can start with that.

CW As Simon said we're part of a Preservation Community and we have people just longing to find a little line like ours to run stock on. There will be a steam loco and a rake of coaches I can promise you.

TH I thought you would have but I like to be sure. And get it all in writing.

SB No question but!

TH You see I believe in this part of world having self-respect. It has its own history, its own industrial heritage if you like -not just part of Manchester.

CW Heartily agree . Our mills were specialist and how many people know there was a coalfield in Northeast Cheshire around Poynton?

TH We don't want to be swallowed up - if you go to southeast England there's towns just swallowed by London -

a whole county - Middlesex - gone. So let's hang on to our heritage.
CW   Indeed!
TH   But hark at me ! Heritage isn't king. Cash is KING
SB   Tell me about it!
TH   I understand you have a three year finance plan. Of course you have! You see I don't want this to go the way of others I've heard of? Near Glossop? At Southport?
SB As I understand it those operations had problems with leases.
TH   Not here you won't. Me or my companies own every speck for miles.
CW   You have clearly done your research Mr Harris.
TH   My former Personal Assistant used to come to you on a Sunday - a regular apparently-
SB   I didn't realise that!
TH   Oh aye - not a volunteer or anything but she brought her kids when that diesel loco was running - not that you'd know that Vicar.
CW   I do tend to be rather busy on Sunday mornings!
TH   She'll have spent a packet on crisps and sweets for those little beggars! Our Betty does an excellent job with stuff from the Cash and Carry. And her scones of course. I tell you - I travel miles for them!
SB   She is an acknowledged asset.
TH   Something for everyone then. That ex-PA of mine - her kids liked riding in that Guards Van - they called it a caboose and they pretended they're in a Western and are being chased by "hostiles"
CW   Ahhh!
TH   And talking of hostiles - what about this opposition? That lady , Miss Izzard, who wrote a nasty letter to the local

paper? I have to tell you that I have personal reasons for not wanting to make enemies round here.

CW I'm not supposed to tell anyone but - Betty doesn't like it to be thought that she eavesdrops -

SB - as if! -

CW   She felt she had to tell me that she had had heard that Miss Izzard who wrote the letter and her cronies who take coffee at her place - she calls them "The Last Of The Summer Wine" - going on a bit - "too loud not to be overheard" - say how much they had been against the enlargement of railway activities. Shades of the Liverpool and Manchester - they thought sparks from a loco would cause fires! Betty apparently said something that made them decide not to attend tonight.

TH   Well done again our Betty! All should go according to the agenda then?

SB   Ruth got the agendas out and they're on the seats for all to see. She's gone back home for the kids but she'll be back in a bit. All straightforward. Vicar will introduce local businessman and chair of the Station Trust and Preservation Society, Mr Simon Buckley who will explain plans for expansion. Then we propose the formation of the East Cheshire Railway Company as a charitable organisation of which I hope you will be a trustee as you are with the existing bodies.

TH   Count on it! But one thing Vicar, before I go and scrounge a cuppa and scone from Betty. When you introduce young Simon here, please will you not do that bit where you say: "The Lord giveth but Doctor Beeching taketh away". Beeching were a businessman for Pete's sake! He was given the job of making Britain's railways profitable and he gave it a go. He had some clever ideas on freight and - think on - if we hadn't ended up with a lot of closed lines you

wouldn't have all these little railways in every corner of the country steaming away and bringing in loads of tourists.
CW   I shall not mention the man at all, I promise
TH   OK. You can count me in as before.
(At that point everyone leaves the stage so let us revert to being a Tale. Ted goes off for cuppa and a scone with Betty in the kitchen and Simon and the Vicar walk together towards the back of the hall.)
As the kitchen door closed on the sizeable figure of Ted Harris, Simon observed: "I think our big man may know more about railways than he pretends. He may not have been wholly open with us when talking about his - did he say - ex-employee. I recognise that person from his description of the kids. Totally wild. There were a danger to themselves. We had to ban them!"
"Interesting also his reaction to possible objections!" added the Reverend Gentleman. "*Not wanting to make enemies* I think he said. Do you think our local philanthropist might just be considering standing for Parliament?"
The sound of laughter from kitchen caused Simon to smile: "It seems our millionaire gets on rather well with Betty!"
"Aha", replied the other. "What I couldn't tell you when he was with us is that Betty is now helping Ted's wife with the list of local invitees to the next Garden Party at The Hall. I know for sure that our Miss Izzard would very much like to be on that list!" He clapped his hands.
"Then let us to the task. Simon - well done so far. With your work - and Ruth's too of course, I know all will go well. I am sure your ancestor will smile down on us and we shall have a GOOD EVENING"

AUTHOR'S POSTSCRIPT

I shall leave to the reader's imagination the proceedings at the Meeting which ensued. Simon's enthusiasm, Rev Warburton's benign suggestion that the Lord is on their side, the beaming affluence of Ted Harris playing the part of the squire, assuring all present that all will be well financially. Miss Izzard would be put firmly in her place suggesting that the re-opened railway would be a hazard to young children. Then the Appeal would be launched and in good spirits all would repair to the Brockleton Arms or the Station Hotel for something stronger.

Fast forward with the imagination to a grand re- opening of the line and the Rev. Warburton on the footplate as the 0-6-0 propels the first train up to Harris Halt.
I would like to think that the line has survived. Perhaps they solved the level crossing problem and extended a further three miles, perhaps now they have a dining car serving luxury Sunday lunches to the well-heeled of northeast Cheshire. Perhaps they have a "Thomas the Tank Engine Day" or a Thursday "Fish and Chips Pensioners' Special" and – who knows? -maybe Ruth might be seen on the footplate of one of the line's steam locos. However things have progressed, one can feel sure that old Sir George would be pleased to see his line being of service.

AUGUST 2018

"Good Evening, Sir George"
The smartly dressed mature woman who had thus accosted Sir George as he was about to exit the Hastings seafront hotel was clearly not hotel staff but she did look familiar to him.
"And Good Evening to you. You have the advantage of me, I'm afraid. Have we met? Should I know you? I must say you look familiar somehow!"
The lady smiled.
"My sister's the Hotel Manager. We DO rather resemble each other. In fact, people often mix us up!"
"Ah! That explains it! And presumably she pointed me out to you – such is the price of a modicum of fame or notoriety."
Sir George was quite sure he had seen the lady before and in his professional capacity. However, he decided not to broach that line of conversation but to continue with the pleasantry of strangers. Years at the Criminal Bar had trained him in the skill of maintaining one line of interchange whilst his mind raced ahead on another.
He smiled and continued.
"My wife and I are down for a short break. Travelled by train – interesting journey."
"Had you not been to Hastings before?"
"No. We decided on this trip as my wife enjoyed the TV Series *Foyle's War* which, as you may know, was filmed here. We've been scouting out some of the locations."
"We have a lot of people doing that!"
"It's quite tiring walking round - my wife is having a lie down actually! We hadn't realised we had arrived in the middle of a Carnival! But it's all very scenic. Do you live in Hastings?"

"St. Leonards."
"I hadn't realised the two towns were contiguous. I'm something of a stranger in East Sussex – though my work has brought me down to Lewes."
Ah that's it! he thought. *She's been involved in something I did at Lewes.*
"Not a place I go to much!"
"Not a place I shall be at again – nor anywhere suchlike. Those days are past now."
She was definitely part of those past days and almost certainly at that business in Lewes but – he had never cross questioned her. No definitely not. So what was it?
The exchange of pleasantries continued.
"You've retired from the Law then?"
"Indeed! The English Bar shall see no more of me. But the wife and I shall see more of England. Starting with Hastings and presumably the adjacent St. Leonards."
"Well worth seeing. A castle, two cliff railways, a fishing fleet and our pier has re-opened - though for how long ? – the downside is that there is a bit of a drink and drugs problem."

Suddenly Sir George remembered a Case that involved residents of Hastings. Memories came flooding back and he could hear once more the voice of his principal witnesses, Dennis and Dilys

* * * * * * * * *

Well, Sir George, we were very pleased when we moved into The Close. The house was new, the Estate was new, a bit far out but there was a bus. We were the first residents in The Close - got out pictures in the local paper too. Soon there were other young couples like us. Early years were fine – we brought up both our daughters there - but everybody seemed to move on and by the time our two girls had left to set up home themselves. it wasn't bright and shiny anymore - far from it. But we stayed on - little chance to do otherwise really and our daughters and the grandkids were an immense joy and the sons-in-law were handy too. You see, Sir George, they were both skilled tradesmen and they could do all of them little repair jobs the Council never seemed to get round to.

His wife had chimed in: *Get to the point Dennis!*

At the time we're talking about then, The Close had gone down a bit and the neighbours weren't what you'd want really. Her across the road was drunk or worse most of the time and her next door - that Tracie - well!

The wife again: *She wasn't what you'd call respectable. never seemed to have a job and had two kids with no sign of a Dad. Oh nice enough - she'd pass the time of day when we were both hanging out the washing round the back. And you should have seen her washing. No respectable woman wears that sort of thing - I'm sure! But it was her men.*

Dennis resumed: *She was never short of company - if you know what I mean, Sir George. But she had two who lived there for a bit. First there was the Scotch lad - Duggie - I could never make out a word he said - some sort of gamekeeper - worked out near Tenterden somewhere - they were always arguing but he left. Went back to Scotland we were told.*

-You should tell Sir George also that people said she walked about the house with no clothes on and so we often had gangs of lads hanging about hoping to catch sight of her - you know what lads are like - Dennis?

-Also - her over the road was always at her upstairs window for the same reason we thought -

–reckoned one day she'd be found in heap at the bottom of her stairs –
-Then this Dave moved in – big car – loudmouth and it wasn't long before the arguments started – banging and shouting at all hours-
- You went round once didn't you Dennis?
-Fat lot of good that did!

Sir George had gently drawn them round to describing the night in question when they had been wakened at around 1.30 a.m. He remembered the couple nervously recalling the sequence of events.

Dennis described the sound as being like a gunshot but could not be sure. [Sir George persuaded him to say he was sure when it came to court!] Then he had looked out of the bedroom window noting that the neighbour opposite was doing likewise. He remembered seeing Dave's car parked as usual at the front but also was surprised to see Duggie's van. He maintained his vigil but just when he was about to re-join his wife there was further activity.

This time Dilys joined him in peering anxiously from their unlighted window. They would always remember what they saw.

Duggie and Tracie were lugging a heavy bundle, it looked like a rolled carpet, out of the house, along the short garden path and out into Duggie's van. Then Duggie got in and drove off.

Not knowing what on earth to make of this, they made themselves a cup of tea and resumed their watch. Their vigilance was rewarded after about half an hour when Tracie reappeared carrying first some luggage and then her two toddlers out to Dave's car and driving off.

They found that further sleep was impossible and sat in their kitchen until the morning when they telephoned both daughters. Dutifully, their concerned offspring dashed to The Close and took it upon themselves to knock on Tracie's front door, then go round the back and peer in through windows from which investigation they concluded there was no-one at home.

At that point they were nonplussed and sat around for some time drinking tea and making suggestions as to what might have happened and then querying as to whether it was any of their business.

Then hours later, there was a knock at the door. The neighbour from across the way seemed the worse for drink but explained that a previous tenant had given her a spare key to Tracie's.

* * * * *

The bell finally rang with Sir George: *That's who I'm talking to!*

"You were the neighbour with the key. You're Nicola. You led the way in."

"Yes indeed and in some trepidation I can tell you! But all we found was the front room in disarray with the carpet gone. All Dave's stuff was there as far as we could see and at that point we called the Police. The rest you know of course."

"And what a case it was too! Brilliant work by the local CID to find Tracie and her chap. He was a gamekeeper in the Scottish Borders and of course he had a gun. The evidence was strong against him."

" From Dennis and Dilys but not me."

Sir George felt a twinge of concern: *Was this the point of her accosting him?* Then he remembered Nicola's condition at the time.

"I didn't dare call you to the stand. The Welsh wizard for the Defence would have made mincemeat of you. He gave everybody else a tough time but his case fell apart with the Forensics showing how they found tiny spots of Dave's blood in the front room and the hallway and on the front step. That did it in the end. We didn't need you."

"I was surprised that you could get a conviction for murder when there wasn't a corpse."

"Perfectly possible, though it was the only one I ever did."

"But we didn't get Tracie."

"As you will possibly remember, the jury believed her story that she had only asked her ex-boyfriend to put the frighteners on her current one, She claimed she had been upstairs with the kids, so all she got was three years for Conspiracy."

"And she'd been on remand for ages so scarcely served any time at all."

Sir George was always quick to spot any prevailing sense of injustice.

"I think Justice was served", he observed in as a kind a manner as he could summon. "The proven killer was duly sentenced. His accomplice in the act lost her home and her family. Was that what you wanted to speak to me about?"

"Well no, actually. A couple of things really. I just had to tell you. Tracie was one of the most beautiful women I ever set eyes on. And she did walk about the house in the nude. She waved to me once from her bedroom window with not a stitch on – set my pulses racing I can tell you! In those days I was the worse for alcohol much of the time and – well I misread the message. When I went across the road to her and – shall we say – made an advance, she reacted in the most violent manner. I'll always remember the look in her eyes that day. I know that she could commit murder, I'll bet she was involved more than we'll ever know!"

"That is often the case in my experience", said Sir George in his practised Senior Partner tone.

"But that's not all", continued Nicola firmly. "When you said you were not going to call me as witness, you also suggested that I seek counselling about my drinking."
"Did I? Good Heavens! That was rather forward of me!"
"It was the best thing that ever happened to me! Sorted me out and nowadays I've a respectable job with an estate agent, a house, car, and a partner. I actually married my counsellor."
"He did a good job then!"
"It's a "she" actually. That turned out to be my problem! Now I know who I am."
"I am delighted for you!"
"So when my sister saw you had booked in here she let me know so I just had to thank you for- indirectly -you changed my life. That's all. You are very welcome in Hastings and I hope you and your lady wife have a GOOD EVENING."

AUTHOR'S POSTSCRIPT

Let me state immediately, lest misconceptions arise, that the homicide rate in the South East Region of England wherein lies the Borough of Hastings, is consistently amongst the lowest in UK, itself a long way down the national "league table" of deaths by homicide per million of population. The Borough Council of this attractive East Sussex seaside town pointed this out during the run of *Foyle's War*, the detective drama television series set during and shortly after the Second World War which ran for eight series from 2002 to 2015. Created by *Midsomer Murders* screenwriter and author Anthony Horowitz, it ran for eight series from 2002 to 2015. The first six series are set during the Second World War in Hastings and fans of the show, such as Sir George's wife in this Tale, are often seen exploring the locality in search of filmed locations. Such quests are aided by the booklet: FOYLE'S HASTINGS; Hastings Borough Council; [2006, Revised 2010] ISBN 0-901536-08-3 but any visitors will soon find that Nicole's list of local attractions in this Tale only skims the surface.

Our Sir George, adopting a magisterial manner, was of course correct when he corrected Nicola's misconception that a "murder trial" could not happen without a corpse. Any search of reference works will quickly provide numerous examples – some notorious -of cases where evidence such as narrated here was sufficient to obtain a conviction.

To end on a happy note: Sir George and his wife had arrived in Hastings during **Old Town Week** when the programme of events does indeed end with a Carnival Procession followed by a firework display in the evening.

OCTOBER 2021

"Good Evening, Sir George."

Having opened the front door in response to the rarely heard tinkling of the bell, Sir George, to his amazement, found himself greeted in chorus by two boys. One was tall, fair haired and blue eyed, the other shorter and darker, both in typical casual teenage dress standing holding bicycles and both looking rather nervous. To his unpractised eye, they looked to be fourteen or fifteen years old and seemed somehow familiar but had they announced themselves as visitors from Mars, he would not have been more surprised. It was not so much that the call had been at the front door which looked out over the canal and was rarely used – all parties preferring the more convenient rear door – but that the callers were young people. This was a class of society with which Sir George normally had no dealing of any sort, his sole offspring being a daughter who, though celebrated in her own way, had indicated she had no intention of joining the ranks of what she described as "breeding females".

He quickly sensed that his level of surprise was matched by his callers' nervousness and so adopted what his friends and family and legal colleagues knew as his "Number One Smile".

"Good evening young gentlemen." He began with a degree of mock formality. "To whom do I have the honour of addressing?"

The taller one answered. "I'm Tadpole. This is Fluebrush."

Maintaining his formality with some difficulty at hearing the rather comic names, Sir George enquired gravely: "And to what does Old Wharf House owe the honour of your visit?"

Before the boys could answer, a voice called from the depths of the modernised 18th Century canal side building:
"Who is it, George?"
His wife having priority at all times; accordingly, he turned from his teenage visitors and, in the act, remembered why they looked familiar.
"It's those two boys who help at the locks in summer, dear", he called to the interior.
"What do they want? We haven't got any jobs."
"Be through in a minute dear. Let you know then."
Having disposed of the marital imperative, Sir George returned his attention to the young visitors.
"I think you may just have heard an answer to a question, gentlemen."
"Gosh" stammered Tadpole. "Yes. Thank you. We'll be on our way then."
But Sir George was not finished and stayed their departure.
"Not so fast! I need to report back to the boss and so I have to have your real names."
"Sorry" both boys chorused, then Tadpole, as was his wont, functioned as spokesman.
"I'm Jeremy Todd Powell and he is Clive Floyd Bruce but everybody calls us Tadpole and Fluebrush."
Sir George nodded, seeing a certain logic.
"Thank you. You clearly know who I am, but everybody round here seems to. I believe I have seen you on your bikes across there". He pointed to the towpath on the other side of the narrow English canal. "I always assumed you were locals from one of the villages who helped boaters through the locks. Are you Sutton Earls or Sutton Abbots?"
"Both actually," replied Tadpole. "I'm from Earls, Fluebrush is an Abbott. "
"I thought the two never spoke!" smiled Sir George.

"We wouldn't have but we met at Prep School and discovered we were from the neighbouring rival villages."
"And how did the rivals come to knock on my door?"
It was the smaller boy's turn to be spokesman.
"It's Tadpole's Ma really. She asked us –"
"–told us" interjected the other –
"–To come to you and ask if there were any jobs we could do for you in the half-term."
[This was a rather condensed account of a lengthy meeting when the boys had been upbraided for a perceived lack of social awareness and their excuse that Sir George and his wife were famous was brushed aside with the remark that famous people still need milk, bread and eggs!]

"That was most kind of her."
Sir George found that he meant it.
Tadpole took up the story.
"Ma always has ideas for hols – once she invited the Manning girls for tea – the older one hates boys and just scowled all the time. The younger one was mad and threw things at Fluebrush . Their Ma had to come and take them home!"

Sir George found he was beginning to warm to these two representatives of a foreign people of whom he had only had bad report. Their attire contained no indication of their school and, his curiosity now aroused by these well-mannered youngsters, Sir George felt encouraged to query further.
"Are you still at the same school?"
Tadpole, as was his wont, began the reply with:
"Not any more sadly. It was the plan ..!"

The other interjected: "... and then my Pa foolishly lost a lot of money in 2008 and I had to go downmarket! Not that I think it will matter in the long run.."
"Our parents don't set much store by education" explained Tadpole.
"It has its uses" smiled Sir George. "It can rather help you in a career."
Tadpole, with Fluebrush nodding furiously in agreement, contended with the air of one who had explained matters to adults oft times before:
"What our families say is that it's not what you're taught that counts, it's where you're taught."

Sir George mentally conceded that the boy might have a point and was keen to hear more but thought it wisest to steer clear of any mention of academic studies. Often in his years at the English Bar, Sir George had remarked to his juniors that success in the Legal Profession comes from knowing what question to ask and when. He now found himself directed by his own guidelines as he remembered from his own youth that "*What do you want to be when you grow up?*" was a question one DID NOT ask teenagers. Thus his next enquiry of his young visitors was: "And to what use do you intend to put this schooling?"

As so often, Tadpole led.
"Our families have always been in the City or the Army."
Fluebrush expanded: " An ever so many greats grandfather fought in the Zulu War - at- Rorke's Drift possibly but without being Welsh!"
Sir George's wife was Welsh and thus he had learnt never to question the historical accuracy of the film *Zulu!* So he let

the moment pass and did not divert the boy from his no-doubt heartfelt pronouncement on Education:

"Pa often says, *'only lesson you need to learn is:* **Don't invest in Property Funds** *and as you won't find a schoolteacher who has the faintest idea of what one of those IS – then it all seems pointless to me!'*"
Sir George smiled. "So which is it for you – City or Army?"
"Oh – City! I shall go into Finance and work hard and get back the family fortune."
Sir George looked at the determination shown on the young face and believed him! He turned his attention to Tadpole.
"Do you share that view of your education?"
"My view," said the boy rather grandly, "Is that it is like taxation – there to be endured."
Sir George laughed – something he had not done for a long time.
"Is that really your view or are you quoting your father also?"
"No, my Pa hardly ever mentions school except to complain about the fees. He did once say that all I needed to know for my career is the case of Carlill versus The Carbolic Smokeball Company – that's all you need to know to be successful as a Contract lawyer!"
Sir George smiled as he recalled the classic exemplar case from his student days. "So you are going into Law? Well, of course, I approve wholeheartedly of that decision," he began and then a thought struck him.
 "Clearly you have family connections in the legal profession but if it seems right at the time, then I am sure a word from me to my old Chambers would see you right."
"Gosh thank you sir", came the reply.
"And the Army tradition? continued Sir George.
"We believe in honouring that," replied Fluebrush.

"We'll be with our families at the Cenotaph on Remembrance Sunday", added Tadpole.

"I am impressed", replied Sir George. "I haven't done that for decades. Always watch on television, of course. Very moving. But well done you youngsters for being there."

Feeling that the discourse had run its time, he decided on one last question.

"And when you have made your fortunes in the worlds of Law and Finance – what then?"

"Oh, travel of course", replied Fluebrush.

"Yes" agreed his companion. "Cricket in Australia" –

– "Rugger in New Zealand or South Africa" continued the other.

"You could perhaps trace that ancestor from the Zulu Wars" commented Sir George, warming to these ideas.

"We did go on a school tour to World War One sites" added Fluebrush. "I think we'd both like to go back there and see some more."

"And my wife will be wanting to see me some too, young gentlemen. I thank you for coming round. My best regards to your parents. Do feel free to offer your services again when you are at home. My wife's health is greatly improved now and we have a daily house help from Sutton Earls and a garden helper from Sutton Abbotts. They don't speak to each other, of course – still not got over being on opposite sides in the Civil War three and a half centuries ago! – but they are very valuable additions to the household and could possibly find something for you."

"Thank you very much" came the reply in chorus and the boys made to wheel their bikes off the premises. Sir George, emboldened by the rapport he felt had built up, felt he could now issue a cautionary note.

"Chaps", he began, "Before you go, just a word. As you may have gathered, I had seen you before. In fact I had noted you several times last summer and once in the last few days. I think it most admirable that you seem interested in the canal - - the country's canals are living history" –
" That exactly what my Ma says", exclaimed Tadpole. "And she gives talks about that sort of thing and visits all sorts of places. SO we DO know a bit about the canals, sir!"
Not to be outdone, Fluebrush chimed in: "And my Ma found a website which told us about cycling along the towpaths. It made sense and we ARE following it now."

Sir George chuckled: "My goodness me, you chaps seem to be properly organised and I am duly instructed by you. My regards to your parents. My wife and I are very touched by their solicitude."

With the fast sinking sun picking out a myriad of tints on the trees of an English autumn, Sir George surveyed his local landscape with a suddenly lightened heart. He had made a chance encounter of the most pleasant kind. Two very pleasant, well-mannered representatives of a class of society he had been given to believe had no interest in anything save mindless selfish pursuits and electronic pastimes had caused him to totally revise that judgement. There was hope for the country after all!

So much had been doom and gloom in the recent months but now his wife seemed on the mend and the late national medical emergency seemed but a memory and it all added up to a GOOD EVENING.

AUTHOR'S POSTSCRIPT

I thought I might add something slightly different and hope I have introduced an upbeat note. In keeping with what my sharpest reviewer has described as an "erudite" content, I shall explain one reference.

No wonder Sir George smiled when the famous 1892 case ***Carlill v Carbolic Smoke Ball Company*** was mentioned and many readers also will have had their memories jogged by reference to a classic decision in Contract Law. This is not the place to go into the oddly named case and its curious subject matter, suffice it to say that thereby we have defined that Offer and Acceptance, Consideration and an Intention to Create Legal Relations are essential elements of a contract. Pretty important then!

Regarding the reported towpath activities of the two young volunteers it would seem that they had been made aware of the guidelines published by the Canal & River Trust www.canalrivertrust.org.uk .

I think I should also point out that the purported opinions on the value of a school education expressed by characters in this Tale are not supported by the author!

ALSO ...if anyone wants to elaborate on the lives of the young protagonists, Tadpole and Fluebrush, please feel free – only DO remember where you met them first!

FEBRUARY 2018

"Good Evening, Sir George. I assume you are up in Edinburgh for the Calcutta Cup game on Saturday."
As only his wife had known he had travelled up early and where he intended to stay over the weekend of the Scotland versus England Rugby International, Sir George was not expecting to meet anyone in the bar of his club and was thus momentarily startled. However his years in the Legal Profession in England had accustomed him to sudden surprises and he instantly assumed his professional equanimity with the smiling rejoinder:
"Indeed and for our traditional Former Pupils Association Dinner which we always have on the Friday before the game. But you must forgive me, I recognise the face but cannot - for the moment put a name to it."
"Dunbar. Sandy Dunbar."
"Ah yes. Young Mr. Dunbar from The Bank."
"Bank no longer, Sir George. For some years I've headed Dunbar Associates."

Now Sir George could place the face although the passage of time had done its sculpture. Some years back his London legal firm had found itself involved in the business of an elaborately constituted charitable trust based in Edinburgh and, although he was qualified as an English lawyer, his partners prevailed upon him to attend some key meetings in his native city. It was soon clear that his was merely a token presence but he had enjoyed the opportunity to meet with former schoolfriends with whom he now met regularly at Murrayfield and Twickenham. A feature of the meetings had been the interjections of a fresh faced young man who far exceeded his brief with descriptions of investment opportunities. He had thought at the time: *This young man will go far.* Clearly he had.

Going through the process at the bar of refreshing their glasses whilst making the usual polite conversation about the weather, he was about to remark upon the coincidence of their meeting again but stopped himself. He had remembered he was in Edinburgh and not London! He was in a much smaller metropolis where business and professional men had established bolt holes that they put in operation in busy times such as International weekends or during the Festival in summer. Then it came to him, it was not just the face that had rung a bell but the name of the firm – Dunbar Associates !

He had heard the name quite recently with regards to the affairs of the late Mr. Tommy Singleton. Silly of him - should have made the connection! Sir George snapped his fingers.

"Now I come to think of it – I did hear of your organisation in connection with a deceased client's estate."

"That would be the redoubtable Mr. Tommy Singleton – *one time soldier, all-time opportunist* I've heard him called. Yes -I did note your practice was handling the matter."

"The gentleman had quite a substantial holding in one of your funds, as I recall. Please don't get me wrong but I thought it an odd choice – rather out of character."

Dunbar smiled.

"There's a bit of a story there as it happens."

"I should imagine so – Tommy Singleton never did anything without good reason. He wasn't given to mistakes!"

"He did make one once – a long time ago."

"Before you were born I should think."

"You've hit the nail on the head, Sir George. Nine months before to be exact."

"Oh don't tell me you're a result of his misspent youth! My practice has been struggling for months with spurious claims on his estate. An amazing number of sworn statements have materialised!"

"I think I may have rather more than that, Sir George."

"You interest me!"

"My late mother wrote to Mr. Singleton just before she died and I have his handwritten reply – a holograph document as you chaps say – in which he says that, whereas he would not acknowledge parenthood, he would make sure that I would be well looked after."

Sir George spotted the trend the conversation was taking.

"There's no good asking me about The Will! But I can tell you that you are mentioned in the accompanying Letter of Wishes."

* * * * * * * * * * * * * * * *

After the two had parted – Sir George pleading an entirely fictitious engagement – and having exchanged business cards, Sir George had a chuckle to himself. He would always remember the greedy look which came upon the younger man's face regarding a possible bequest. How would he react when he found out that all Tommy Singleton had left his natural son was his regimental tie!

Well, thought Sir George, *so far, this has been a GOOD EVENING.*

AUTHOR'S POSTSCRIPT

I could scarcely leave my collection of Tales without a mention of the Calcutta Cup, that annual contest at the game of Rugby Union Football between Scotland and England which dates from 1879 At the time of this Tale, England had won NINE successive matches. That was to change on the Saturday following the related encounter so we can imagine the delight [and general roistering] of Sir George and his former schoolmates!

On legal matters:

The legal systems of Scotland and of England and Wales have remained separate, so our London-based Sir George, whilst clearly very senior in his profession, would not necessarily be considered qualified in Scotland!

More germane to our Tale: A **Letter of Wishes** is a convenient tool that can be used by someone making a Will to give guidance to its administrators. Attractions are that it can be relatively informal and can be changed at any time and also its contents do not have to be made public.

I leave you with the thought: *Was it REALLY a coincidence that the acquisitive young Mr Dunbar – he of the enquiring mind – had encountered the Head of the legal firm handling his natural father's will?*

JANUARY 2018

Being my transcription of an audio recording with redactions dated 25th January 2018 which came to me by a roundabout route. It opens with few seconds of unidentified sounds and inaudible speech. Then comes the readily identifiable sound of knocking on a door accompanied by a female voice saying: "It IS them". We hear a door opening followed by male voices in unison.

-Good evening, Sir George
-Good evening gentlemen. Do please come in and take a chair. Thank you both for coming. *Great deal of furniture noise.* I realise that this is an unconventional venue but given that your Interparliamentary Committee meets tomorrow morning and your communications to my office over the past few days indicated an element of urgency, I felt that convening here – informal as it may be – would move matters quickly. *Unidentified voices indicate assent.* May I introduce Ms Purvis - that's Papa Uniform Romeo Victor India Sierra – from MoD who you may have contacted in the past and issued the official reply to this ridiculous allegation and the almost legendary Taffy Griffiths who - unlike any of us -has actually been to the site at the heart of the matter. *Babble of greetings. Same voice continues.*
This will not- indeed must not - take long for as you may well deduce from my attire, I have a Dinner Engagement shortly, two floors down and I know Taffy and Ms Purvis also have functions to attend. This is not a secure venue but you will see that is of no matter. We should not be interrupted but I understand there is a Scots piper staying across the hallway. Now everybody, we are agreed there is but one item on the agenda – are we not? *Various murmurs that we can assume signify assent.* It is of course, the sudden

appearance last week in a UK-wide tabloid newspaper – albeit tucked away in the inside pages –of an article which accused the MoD of storing nuclear warheads in an English country village.

The microphone picks up mutterings discernible as "Exactly" and "Precisely" and the same voice continues.

Now everybody here knows exactly where UK nuclear warheads are stored and, as we are not in a secure environment, I shall not mention any names. But – and this is why we are assembled at such short notice – the article was spotted by those whose job it is to do so and alarms sounded in the corridors of power. The reverberations , of course, reached my desk and compelled action. So, I will start, if I may, by updating you on actions taken by the Security Services. *More mutterings of assent and more of the same voice.*

Right then – on the day after the article appeared complete with the carefully crafted counter from Ms Purvis, officers visited the Editor of the newspaper in question. I have their report here – which I can pass over for parliamentary scrutiny – it suggests a jocular meeting. It appears that a young ambitious reporter *VERY LONG BLEEP* but the Editor being a canny old bird who is no stranger to wild allegations and their legal ramifications, decided to hold fire and contacted Ms Purvis first. You will have noted that the article in question contains no placenames and wasn't given a by-line. *General mumbled assent and we can hear Ms Purvis saying "Absolutely!"*

Updating you further – the aforementioned officers in the Security Service being duly informed by the extremely co-operative Editor, paid a visit to young Mister BLEEP

BLEEP the journalist who started all this. He duly admitted to staying overnight at The BLEEP in BLEEP BLEEP with a travelling companion.

- *Someone says "Hmmmmm"*
- When asked how he came to believe the site was a nuclear weapons store he tells of a conversation with locals. I have his Statement here gentleman – a copy of which you may take with you – and I quote from it:
- First Local: I came past the secret base this morning – there was someone working there
- Second local: I expect they were checking up on the nuclear warheads.

Our intrepid reporter queried these local chaps who must then have begun the Old English sport of misleading visitors but his curiosity was aroused and the following morning, he states, he drove down the road to BLEEP BLEEP and did indeed see, in the woods beside the road a massive fence and big gates with the sign: MoD PROPERTY KEEP OUT. Under further questioning, according to the report, young Mr BLEEP – in my opinion rattled by this turn of events - admitted he has no tangible evidence concerning a nuclear weapons establishment He further agreed that the locals may have been pulling his leg. He also made a plea that the matter be not taken further. The unofficial opinion of the agents who questioned him was that his companion may not have been whom she purported to be.

Sound of what may be taken to be sniggering. Speaker continues.

Now, whilst that would seem to be the end of the matter, it occurred to me that slamming the book shut at this point might well be construed by some as a cover-up. Hence I contacted the two persons who are with us this evening and who may be taken as "Expert Witnesses". So let us first hear about the site in question from Ms Purvis.

-Thank you Sir George. If I may explain that I had previously researched the history of this strange parcel of land which I am sure is germane to our agenda.

One of the visitors can be picked up saying: "By all means."
This small, wooded site was donated to the then Air Ministry in late nineteen forty by Lord BLEEP BLEEP in recognition - it would seem - for the part played by the Royal Air Force the previous summer - I'm sure I don't have to explain that.
Muttered agreement. The lady continues.
My belief is that His Lordship intended this pleasant little area to become a war cemetery. I think he wanted it to be like that place near Mons we visited when I was at school.
Taffy: St Symphorien?
Sir George: A bonnie spot indeed. My favourite of all those First World War Cemeteries.
-Oh absolutely! But of course it never happened that way! Our site, in 1941, was developed after that strange episode when Rudolf Hess landed and it was decided to set up a safe site for VIP prisoners. Actually I don't think Hess was ever there but it was used in 1944 to house troops earmarked for D-Day who had gone AWOL and other persons deemed likely to spread "careless talk". And that is the highest height of its fame. Very pleasant little spot it would seem. Somehow it got the nickname "Dingley Dell". It's just used as a surplus store. Gosh - I think that's all, Sir George.

- Thank you Ms Purvis. A very impressive piece of historical research if I may say.

-I did read History at Cambridge!

-We are the better for it! Gentlemen can I now introduce my other "expert", Major Griffiths. You may have come across contributions from him before but shall I summarise that, after a distinguished career in the British Army, he has become a much-in-demand premises security specialist. There are few military sites where he has not advised on their security and his remit has included landmarks such as Buckingham Palace and the Bank of England! Taffy - the floor is yours.

- Thank you Sir George and thank you for bringing me into this matter -a shame we have had to crowd this meeting into this busy evening. By a coincidence, I visited Dingley Dell last October. It is a very strange set-up and I was greatly obliged to Ms Purvis for digging into its history for me and, of course, that work has been doubly useful. I included it in my report of the time and I can pass to you the relevant extract. The cub reporter commented on the surprisingly strong security fencing at the site and I can certainly confirm that. The reason for it derives not from the present use but from the history that you just heard. A fence designed to keep people in can be just as useful keeping people out! That might well have been part of the design as I understand from Ms Purvis, there was a suggestion that Polish troops stationed in UK planned to break into a site where Hess was imprisoned and assassinate him!

Various exclamations suggesting surprise to which Taffy assents before continuing.

Now all of you will be asking the question I asked when I did my survey last year - why the heck is this place still open? Is there something secret about it? Now I am but a simple soldier and can't give you chapter and verse but - a huge but - there's a legal problem. You will recall Ms Purvis said earlier that the site had been gifted to the Air Ministry and it appears that there is something irrevocable about the gift. So it is easier for the Ministry of Defence to keep this place open that it would be to try and close it ... Sir George?

-It occurs to me that this must be a situation very like one which my cousin in Northeast Cheshire - er - Manchester-is always banging on about. There is a railway station thereabouts which is deemed surplus to requirements by the Train Operators but which is more trouble to close than to use – so they keep it open with the absolute minimal service, one train a week.

Somebody says: "Good Heavens!" then Taffy concludes
-I can report to you that Dingley Dell is nothing more than a clothing store. Oh Ms Purvis has something on that ..
-I did get my hands on a supply inventory – a copy of which you may have – it's not exactly Top Secret – if you have a look - there was a delivery probably the one the locals saw – the most surprising thing is the amount of socks!

Great deal of noise of paper then some chuckles and Sir George continues.
-So all this to-do has been caused by someone seeing a delivery of surplus military socks and a silly young man – on some illicit sexual adventure – misinterpreting.
So we have spent time over a delivery of surplus socks which, if drawn to the attention of Press or parliament, is likely to raise howls of merriment and derision which we all wish to avoid.

Murmurs of assent.
- Gentlemen you have all the evidence you need to point out to the Honourable Members that this whole thing is a load of nonsense and that your distinguished Committee has far more serious matters to consider. For my part – this matter is now closed and there is nothing further to say.

Confused babble of noise where the listener can just about hear sentiments of agreement followed by furniture noise where we can assume the visitors leave the room. The subsequent speech is quite faint but we can hear Sir George:

-Well folks that is an end to that! Thank you both again for your excellent efforts. Ms Purvis, I must apologise for not recognising your academic background.
-Oh gosh think nothing of it, Lovely to be of some real use.
-Taffy, your presence gave an official air to proceedings and certainly seemed to impress our visitors who - incidentally could have been a bit more forthcoming with the thanks.
The next bit is very faint. It occurs to me the pair of you could put research together and publish a history of Dingley Dell!
No audible reply.
Let us be off then. I trust you will both have an enjoyable end to your day and I for one intend to have a GOOD EVENING.

There is a click and the rest is silence but of course you will be expecting some comments, as is my custom , so here is the:

AUTHOR'S POSTSCRIPT

The above came into my possession whilst this collection of trivia was in preparation. The donor was a declared fan of the "Sir George" books who thought I might like to include it. There was one proviso: that I should make it clear that the two named persons – she of the plummy voice and he of the legendary status of which I must declare my previous ignorance - did NOT have a mutual assignation on that evening or any other!
I must state that I had no recollection of the report appearing in the tabloid press in UK at that time – I was very busy working on my family memoir *Other Times, Other Places* – and it would seem that this extremely minor incident has faded from public memory also.

I have little to do with Military History these days but I get several emailed circulars and none of them have suggested that a history of "Dingley Dell" has ever appeared. I assume that the site is still in use and anyone not privy to its whereabouts might wish to do some detective work as to its location. So by way of help, I can reveal that the bleeping is not as complete as my transcription might suggest and that both the adjoining villages may have names beginning with "Aston" with the pub being either The Bell" or "The Bull".

I should also point out that that this Sir George has a marked Scottish accent and that would explain his haste to get away to an event on the evening of 25th January, which - for the unenlightened - is the anniversary of the birth of the Scottish National Bard, Robert Burns!

ASIDES ABOUT ASIDES

I

Had I not visited this very emotive site, I would not have been able to decipher the name: St Symphorien. This Commonwealth War Graves Commission Military Cemetery is located 1.5 miles or 2 km east of Mons on the N90, a road leading to Charleroi. The German Army established the cemetery and it contains the graves of both German and Commonwealth soldiers, mostly victims of the Battle of Mons [23rd August 1914]. I remember it particularly as it contains the graves of Private John Parr, of the 4th Battalion, Middlesex Regt, and George Lawrence Price of the Canadian 28th (Northwest) Battalion, each believed to be the respective first and last Commonwealth soldiers killed in action during the First World War.

II

Despite having on my walls the framed preambles to Acts of Parliament under GEORGII IV. REGIS of May 1829 and May 1830 concerning the Warrington and Newton Railway – decorative offshoots of my research for Chapter X of *Good Afternoon, Sir George* – I do not identify as a "Railway Buff". Those who do thus class themselves must forgive any inaccuracies in the following.

You will remember Sir George interrupting Taffy with a remark about a railway station which I believe I can identify as Reddish South, a stop on the Stockport–Stalybridge Line in Reddish, Stockport, England. One of the quietest on the UK rail network, it has acquired cult status and at the time of this Tale received only one service per week, the minimum statutory service level required to avoid starting formal closure proceedings.

Matters may have changed for the better– do let me know.

and a COMMENT

We have been made privy to a clearly clandestine recording of proceedings at an unofficial meeting which occurred on 25th January 2018 and at a hotel "Somewhere in London". It is not difficult to work out who made the recording but what I have so far not mentioned is that it was of dreadful quality! Hence I had considerable difficulty with the transcription; for example I was very glad to have the lady's surname spelled phonetically!

The savvy readers amongst you will now be saying: Why did you not use one of the many software tools which would have done the transcribing automatically. To that I would make two points in my defence:
- This contribution arrived just as I was completing this book and, with deadlines to meet, I had no time to investigate the market in transcription software;
- What I have not mentioned is that the audio had a high level of extraneous noise and I do not have the skills to edit that out – if that indeed be possible. There was a constant shuffling of papers and tinkling of glasses of water, one of the participants clearly had all the symptoms of the common cold [not unusual in UK in January!] and I do not know what that type of software would make of the scraping of chairs- one occasion producing an ear shattering scream!

Despite all that, as in Chapter IX in *Good Afternoon, Sir George,* I thought it was a comical piece to include and that the security of the Realm was not endangered by it being tagged on to a collection of fictional Tales. It might have seemed churlish not to so do -I trust you will agree!

ENDPIECE

The above is a scan taken from an original pencil sketch in the artist's unpublished sketchbook which he entitled: *Shadows Of The Evening At "The Pines" Katanning West Australia* and signed *R.S.Y. July 1931.*

The monogram is that of Robert Scott Yule and it has appeared before, on p79 of my *Other Times, Other Places* [see over the page] where you can read - if you have not already done so - about who the artist was and why he was in Western Australia.

The title and the mood of the work suggested it as suitable endpiece.

OTHER TIMES, OTHER PLACES is a book based on the unique diaries kept by two unremarkable, young Scots at two separate times on two different sojourns in two different continents in the 1930's. The two Scots are the author's Mum and Dad whose observations of travel to and life in Western Australia and then Sierra Leone give a fascinating glimpse of a vanished era. The modern reader is given a picture of the background of both Diarists in industrial central Scotland and of the society which shaped their attitudes to the pioneering culture where they found themselves. Acclaimed for its comprehensive research and explanatory notes, the book includes hitherto unpublished sketches and rarely seen photographs and the cooperation of Family and Industrial Historians has enabled the inclusion of current illustrations of those scenes.

250 pp softback ISBN 978-1-787823-285-3
[Andrew Donald Yule Imprint of CompletelyNovel.com, 2019]

Obtainable through Amazon, Barnes & Noble etc

First in the Sir George *Series*

GOOD MORNING, SIR GEORGE

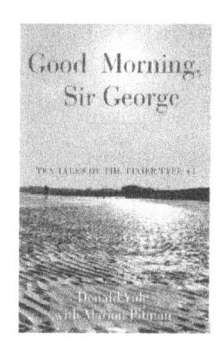

One day during the 2019 County Cricket Season, Donald Yule remarked to his friend, Marion Pitman, that the chap who had walked past them in the famous pavilion at Lord's Cricket Ground looked like he ought to be called "Sir George". When circumstances suggested that Donald invent stories to publish in a wee book which would raise money for charity, the time seemed ripe for a number of "Sir George" characters to appear in print. So in this collection are ten "tiny tales" all with a different Sir George and mostly set against a background of historical events or circumstances. Making up the XI is a previously unpublished piece from the very Marion Pitman, who happily is an acclaimed short story writer.

So here, to pass an idle hour, you may find a different take on: how *Coronation Street* was born; the story behind R L Stevenson's *Kidnapped;* how Arthur Ransome created *Swallows & Amazons* and other similar diversions.

112 pp softback ISBN 978-1-78723-456-7
[Andrew Donald Yule Imprint of Ingram Spark, 2020]
Obtainable through Amazon, Barnes & Noble etc

Second in the Sir George *Series*
GOOD AFTERNOON SIR GEORGE?

Following the welcome for the Ten Tiny Tales which all featured different characters having only their name and title in common, here are ten more off the same production line. Well - perhaps not exactly ten for the savvy reader may well spot a second appearance from one who featured in *Good Morning, Sir George*! Once again these Tales have a real-life location or are set against a background of historical events. As time has moved on since the first appearance of a phalanx of similarly titled personages, so has the time of day of each Tale altered and all our occasions and greetings are post noon.

So here, to pass an idle hour, you may find a different take on: how one of Britain's' favourite snacks acquired its trademark addition; how a noted children's author got an idea for one of her books and how a famous Second World War fighter bomber was conceived. All that and other diversions including one "Sir George" who doesn't say a single word!

114 pp softback ISBN 978-1-52728-875-1
[Sandra Jane Donaldson Yule Imprint of Ingram Spark, 2021]
Obtainable through Amazon, Barnes & Noble etc

Not quite "Goodbye Sir George " just yet. One more dialogue ...

A TIMELESS FRAGMENT

- Good Evening, Sir George.
-Sorry Bill - must dash - off to the opera with Alicia - taxi's just arrived.
-OK - tomorrow lunch?
-OK - this isn't a good line - where and when?
-Mucky Duck 12.30-ish - whoever's first grabs a table in the corner - -and orders the pork pies.
- Right oh! Must go young man - coming darling!

* * * * * * * * * * * * * * * * *

-Ah you beat me to it, young Bill - and the pies - well done! White Swan speciality.
-Sit down and make yourself comfortable, sir. We should be OK here - that noisy young lot from over the road aren't in yet and I got you a pint of your favourite.
-Indeed and if it weren't illegal- I would think you were trying to bribe me!
- As if! How was the opera?
- Not my scene as you know - and with that lot I keep fancying I'm hearing a Welsh accent
-Like at the rugby club?

-Exactly - but Alicia's cousin's daughter was supposed to be in the chorus - damned if we could pick her out!
-Not surprised with all the stage make up. This beer's in good nick. Cheers!
- Cheers! Look Bill -oh! Alicia sends her love to you and Gwen by the way. What's this all about - if it's confidential in any way, we can't really chat in here - not with the eyes and ears of the world sat over in the corner there- and the beggar recognised me.
-Sir George - you know me - I'm not one for gossip but this time - well - it's the absolute END!

.. which of course, it is!

Thank you for reading these Tales and indulging an octogenarian's whims.